**KU-203-135**

To the wonderful team at
Mills & Boon Modern/Harlequin Presents.

I've had the privilege of working with
several editors in London and they've all been
fabulous and supportive.

Thank you for turning my imaginings into these
iconic books with the red banner and circled embrace.

It's a dream come true! Xo

# CLAIMING HIS CHRISTMAS WIFE

## DANI COLLINS

**MILLS & BOON**

First Published in Great Britain 2018
by Mills & Boon, an imprint of HarperCollins*Publishers*
1 London Bridge Street, London, SE1 9GF

© 2018 Dani Collins

ISBN: 978-0-263-93507-3

MIX
Paper from
responsible sources
FSC® C007454

This book is produced from independently certified FSC™ paper
to ensure responsible forest management.
For more information visit www.harpercollins.co.uk/green.

Printed and bound in Spain
by CPI, Barcelona

# CHAPTER ONE

"MR. *TRAVIS* SANDERS?"

"Yes," he confirmed shortly, willing the woman to hurry to the point. His PA had interrupted a high-level meeting with this "extremely important" call. "What is this about?"

"Imogen Gantry. She's your wife?"

Memory washed through him in a rush of heat and hunger. He tensed against it and glanced around, lowering his voice. That broken teacup had been swept firmly under the rug four years ago.

"We're divorced. Are you a reporter?"

"I'm trying to locate her next of kin. I'm at…" She mentioned the name of one of New York's most beleaguered public hospitals.

Whatever old anger had sent him soaring at the mention of his ex-wife exploded in a percussive flash. He was blind. Falling. Wind whistling in his ears. Air moving too fast for him to catch a gulp.

"What happened?" he managed to grit out. He was dimly aware his eyes were closed, but she was right there in front of him, laughing. Her green eyes glimmered with mischief. Her hair was a halo of flames licking at her snowy complexion. She swerved her lashes to cut him a glance. So enchantingly beauti-ful. Gaze clouding with arousal. Sparking with anger. Looking so wounded and vulnerable that last time he'd seen her, his heart still dipped thinking of it.

He'd quickly learned it was a lie, but that didn't make any of this easier to accept.

Gone? He couldn't make it fit in his head. He had told her he never wanted to see her again, but discovered he had secretly believed he would.

From far away, he heard the woman say, "She collapsed on the street. She's feverish and unconscious. Do you know of any medication we should be aware of? She's awaiting treatment, but—"

*"She's not dead?"*

He heard how that sounded, as if that was the outcome he would have preferred, but leave it to Imogen to set him up to believe one thing, contort his emotions to unbearable degrees, then send him flying in another direction. That betraying, manipulative— If he could get his hands on her, he'd kill her himself.

"And she was taken to *that* hospital? *Why?*"

"I believe we were closest. She doesn't seem to have a phone and yours is the only name I've been able to find in her bag. We need guidance on treatment and insurance. Are you able to provide that?"

"Contact her father." He walked back toward the door to his office, saying to his PA behind her desk, "Look up Imogen Gantry's father. He's in publishing. Maybe starts with a *W.* William?" He hadn't met the man, only heard her mention him once or twice. Hell, they'd only been married fifteen minutes. He knew next to nothing about her.

"Wallace Gantry?" His PA turned her screen. "He

appears to have died a few months ago." She pointed to the obit notice that said he was predeceased by his wife and eldest daughter, survived by his youngest daughter, Imogen.

Perfect.

He knew better than to let himself get sucked back into her orbit, but what else could he say except, "I'll be there as soon as I can."

Imogen remembered sitting down on the curb. It hadn't been a nice, rain-washed boulevard of freshly mown grass beneath century-old elms with a stripe of side-walk, then an empty canvas of manicured lawn to her mother's rose garden, ending at the wide stairs to the double-door entrance of her childhood home.

No, it had been a freezing, filthy inner-city curb where the piles of snow had turned to a layer of lumpy muck atop a century's worth of chewing gum and other disgusting things. The damp chill on the air hadn't squelched any of the terrible smells coming off the grate at her feet. She shouldn't have touched the post she had braced herself against and she had thought a car would likely run over her legs as she sank down. At the very least, one would drown her with a tsunami of melt from the puddles.

She hadn't cared. The side of her head had felt like it was twice as big as the rest. Her ear, plugged and aching, had begun screaming so loud the sound had been trying to come out her mouth.

She had tried to pretend she didn't have an ear infec-tion because those were for children. Her sister had got them, not her. She hadn't gone swimming recently. She hadn't known how it could have happened, but there she'd been like a damned toddler, nearly fainting with the agony of it, dizzy and hot and sick.

She'd had to sit down before she fell down. A fever was nature's way of killing a virus, so why hadn't this run its course? And who passed out from such a silly thing, anyway?

Her vision had dimmed at the edges, though. She had felt so awful she hadn't cared that the wet snow had been soaking through her clothes. Her only thought had been, *This is how I die.* She'd been okay with it. Her father would have loved this for her, dying like a dog in the gutter a week before Christmas. Even Travis would probably conclude that she had got what she deserved. If he ever found out, which he wouldn't.

It had been a relief to succumb. Fighting was hard, especially when it was a losing battle. Giving up was so much easier. Why had she never tried it before?

So, she had died.

Now she was in—well, this probably wasn't heaven, not that she expected to get in *there.* It might be hell. She felt pretty lousy. Her body ached and her sore ear felt full of water. The other one was hypersensitive to the rustle of clothing and a distant conversation that bounced painfully inside her skull. Her mouth was so dry she couldn't swallow. She tried to form words and all she could manage was a whimper of misery.

Something lifted off her arm, a warm weight she hadn't recognized was there until it was gone, leaving her with a profound sense of loss. She heard footsteps, then a male voice.

"She's waking up."

*She knew that voice.* Her eyes prickled and the air she'd been breathing so easily became dense and hard to pull in. Her chest grew compressed with dread and guilt. She couldn't move, but inwardly she shrank.

She had definitely gone to hell.

A lighter, quicker footstep came toward her. She opened her eyes, winced at the brightness, then squinted at a tastefully sterile room in placid colors that could have been the one her father had occupied the last months of his life. A private hospital room. For an ear infection? Seriously? Just give her the pink stuff and send her on her way.

"I—" *I can't afford this*, she tried to say.

"Don't try to talk yet," the kindly nurse said. Her smile was stark white and reassuring against her dark brown skin. She took up Imogen's wrist to check her pulse, the nurse's hand soft and warm. Motherly. She checked her temperature and said, "Much better."

All the while, Imogen could almost but not quite see him in her periphery. She was afraid to turn her head on the pillow and look right at him. It was going to hurt and she just didn't have it in her yet.

"How am I here?" she managed to whisper.

"Water?" The nurse used a bendy straw, the kind Imogen had never been allowed to use because they were too common. A gimmick.

She got two gulps down her parched throat before the nurse said, "Easy now. Let me tell the doctor you're awake, then we'll give you more and maybe something to eat."

"How long...?"

"You came in yesterday."

A day and a half in a place like this? When her bank balance was already a zombie apocalypse running rivers of red?

The nurse walked out, sending a smile toward the specter on the other side of the bed.

Imogen closed her eyes again. So childish. She was that and many more things that were bad. Maybe her father was right and she was, simply and irrevocably, *bad*.

A shoe scuffed beside the bed. She felt him looming over her. Heard him sigh as though he knew she was avoiding him the only way she could.

"Why are you here?" she asked, voice still husky. She wanted to squirm. In her most secretive dreams, this meeting happened on neutral turf. Maybe a coffee shop or somewhere with a pretty view. She would have had a cashier's check in hand to pay him back every cent she'd been awarded in their divorce settlement—money she knew he felt she'd conned out of him. Somehow, in her fantasy, she found the words to explain why she'd taken it and he had, if not forgiven her, at least not despised her any longer.

Maybe his feelings toward her weren't that bad. He was here, wasn't he? Maybe he cared a little. Had he been worried for her?

She heard a zipper, which made her open her eyes out of curiosity—

Oh, *no*.

"You went through my things?" She clamped her eyes shut against the small red change purse that had belonged to her mother. It held Imogen's valuables— her driver's license, her debit card, her room key, the only photo she had of her with her sister and mother, and the marriage certificate stating Travis Sanders was her husband.

"The nurse was looking for your next of kin." Oh,

this man had a way with disdain. It dripped from a voice which was otherwise deep and warm with an intriguing hint of Southern charm.

She was a connoisseur of disparaging tones, having experienced a lot of them in her lifetime. Neighbors. Teachers. Daddy dearest. Inured as she ought to be, this man cut into her with scalpel-like precision with his few indifferent words.

*He* didn't care if he was the only person left in this world whom she had any connection to. He found his brief association with her abhorrent when he thought about her at all.

"It's my only other piece of identification."

"Birth certificate?" he suggested.

Burned after an argument with her father ages ago. *So* childish.

She wanted to throw her arm over her eyes and continue hiding, but her limbs were deadweights and the small twitch of trying to lift her arm made her aware of the tube sticking out of it.

She looked at the IV, the ceiling, *him*.

Oh, it hurt so badly. He had somehow improved on perfection, handsome features having grown sharper and more arrogantly powerful. He was clean-shaven, not ruggedly stubbled and human-looking the way she remembered him when she dared revisit their shared past—hair rumpled by her fingers, chest naked and hot as he pressed her into the sheets.

Whatever warmth she had ever seen in him had been iced over and hardened. He wore a tailored three-piece suit in charcoal with a tie in frosted gray. His mouth, capable of a sideways grin, was held in a short, stern firmness. Flat gray eyes took in what must appear like soggy laundry dumped out of the washer before it had even been through the rinse cycle. That's about how appealing she felt. While he was...

*Travis.*

Just thinking his name made her throat flex in an agony of yearning. Remorse.

Why was she always in the wrong? Why was she always falling down and getting messy and driving people away when all she wanted was for someone, anyone, to love her just a little? Especially the people who were supposed to.

Oh, she really was a mess if she was going to get all maudlin like that.

*Pull it together, Immy.*

"Is there someone I should call?" Flat silver dollars, his eyes were. When she had met him, she had thought his gray eyes remarkable for being so warm and sharp. The way he had focused his gaze on her had been more than flattering. It had filled up a void of neglect inside her.

Today they were as emotionless and cold as her father's ice-blue eyes. She was nothing to Travis. Absolutely nothing.

"You've done enough," she said, certain he was the reason she was in this five-star accommodation. She flicked her gaze to the window. Snow was falling, but the view was likely a blanket of pristine white over a garden of serenity.

"You're welcome," he pronounced derisively.

Oh, was she supposed to thank him for saving her life by further impoverishing what was left of it?

"I didn't ask you to get involved." She ignored the fact that she kind of had, carting around their marriage certificate instead of their divorce papers. *Where had those ended up*, she wondered.

"Oh, this is on me," he said with unfettered scorn. "I came here thinking—well, it doesn't matter, does it? I made a mistake. *You*, Imogen, are the only mistake I have ever made. Do you know that?"

# CHAPTER TWO

TRAVIS HEARD HER breath catch and watched her eyes widen in surprise at how ruthlessly he'd thrown that direct hit.

He didn't feel particularly bad about knocking her when she was down. He was speaking the truth, and she was showing an annoying lack of appreciation for his helping her when he could have hung up at the sound of her name.

He should have. Imogen Gantry was the epitome of a clichéd, spoiled New York princess. Self-involved, devious and intent on a free ride.

She didn't look like much right now, of course. What the hell had she been up to that she had wound up in an overcrowded, understaffed emergency room, unable to speak for herself?

"Be happy I had you transferred. Do you know where they took you, when they scraped your frozen body off the sidewalk? What were you doing in that part of the city anyway?"

"If I told you, you wouldn't believe me." Her green eyes met his briefly, glimmering with indecision as she wavered toward telling him something, then decided against it. The light in her gaze dimmed and she looked away.

Drugs, he had surmised darkly when he'd heard where she'd been picked up and seen how gaunt she was. It seemed the only explanation. Blood tests hadn't found anything, however. No track marks or withdrawal symptoms, either.

She'd been raging with fever, though. Had a terrible ear infection that had thankfully responded to the intravenous antibiotics. It was something that should have been dealt with sooner, the doctor had said. She could have lost her hearing or wound up with meningitis. He'd looked at Travis as though it was his fault she was so ill.

That had been when she'd been transferred here to this enormously better-equipped private hospital. Travis had been trying to remember her birthday and searching for her details online only to discover she didn't seem to exist anywhere but in the flesh. He'd found a handful of very old posts, selfies with other socialites at whichever clubs had been the it spot around the time they'd married, but aside from her father's obituary, which was short and stated no service would be held, there was nothing recent about her online.

Her father's house had been sold, he quickly discovered, and Travis hadn't been able to find her current address. He'd had to write down his own. He had acted like her husband and approved her treatment, underwriting the cost. What else was he supposed to do?

Whatever they'd given her for the pain had knocked her out for almost twenty-four hours. Given how bedraggled she'd looked, he'd deduced she needed the sleep.

She still had dark circles around her eyes and an olive tinge in her normally ivory face. The hollows in her cheeks he put down to some women's desire for a skeletal frame in the name of fashion, but she was overdue for a manicure and her hair was limp and dull.

Looking at her, all he felt was pity at her condition. Tired anger. He had known he was making a mistake even as he married her, so why had he gone through with it?

The doctor came in at that moment, along with the nurse who elevated her bed. The doctor wanted her to finish her course of antibiotics orally and said she was anemic. Needed iron.

"You're run-down. Burnt out. I'm prescribing a few weeks off work, along with high-potency multivitamins and proper eating. Get your strength back."

*"Off" from what?* Travis wondered acridly. She hadn't held down a real job in her life.

"Thanks," Imogen said with a tight smile, folding the prescription in half once, then held out her hand to Travis.

He gave her the worn silk bag that was all she'd had on her when she collapsed, like she was some kind of runaway. It might have been good quality twenty or thirty years ago, but it was frayed and faded now. Ugly.

"So, I can go?" She indicated the needle still feeding medication and fluids into her arm.

"Oh, goodness no," the doctor said. "You'll have another dose of antibiotics and an iron infusion. We'll talk tomorrow about discharge, but I would think later in the week—"

"I can't afford this," she cut in. "Please." She lifted her arm. "I'd rather you remove this even if I have to pay for it. I'm squeamish."

"Mrs. Sanders—"

"Gantry," she said at the same time Travis said, "We're divorced."

The doctor sent a perplexed look between them.

"My ex-husband isn't paying for my treatment. I am."

Travis had to raise his brows at that, but was far less surprised by her next words.

"And I can't. So." She crossed her arm over her body toward the nurse. "Please get me out of here as quickly and cheaply as possible."

"You're not well," the doctor said firmly. "She's not," he insisted to Travis, causing an annoying niggle of concern to tug on his conscience.

Why did she get to him like this?

Her stupid arm was too heavy to hold up and even her head needed to flop back against the pillow. "Is this pro bono, then?"

She knew it wasn't. She knew suggesting it put Travis in a tight spot. He'd brought her here. He would be liable if she refused to pay.

"I'll pay for her treatment," Travis ground out, tone so thick with contempt she cringed. His next words, resounding with sarcasm, sawed right through her breastbone to scratch themselves into her heart. "You can pay me back."

"I'll pay for my own treatment," she said, capable of her own pointed disdain. If she knew nothing else, she knew that she would not go deeper into his debt. "But my bills stop now. Bring me whatever forms I need to fill out and get this needle out of my arm. Where are my clothes?"

"I threw them away," Travis said.

"Are you serious? Who— Well, that's just great, isn't it? Thanks." She looked at the nurse. "I'll need some pajamas. Heck, throw in a hot meal, since I'm spending like a drunken sailor anyway."

"Like an Imogen Gantry," Travis corrected under his breath, just loud enough for her to hear it.

She glared at him. "Don't let me keep you."

He had the nerve to look at the doctor and jerk his head, ordering the man to confer with him outside the room.

"Don't you talk about me," she said to their backs. "Did you see what just happened?" she asked the nurse.

"Let's finish this dose of medication before we talk about removing your needle. I'll bring you some soup."

Imogen fell asleep in the time it took the nurse to come back, but felt a little better after a bowl of soup and a glass of vegetable juice. Half her weakness in the street had been hunger, she realized. Apparently, the human body needed to eat every day, and sneaking a few maraschino cherries from the bar while she scrubbed the floor behind it didn't count. #ThingsThe yDon'tTeachYouInSchool.

The nurse removed her needle after giving her some pills to swallow, then helped her shower and dress in a pair of drawstring pajamas and a T-shirt with yellow birds on it.

After all that activity, even finger-combing her hair was too much. Imogen used a rubber band she begged off the nurse to gather her wet hair into a messy lump, then sat in the chair, trembling with exertion, pretending she was fully on the mend, fishing for the thin slippers that would no doubt cost her a hundred dollars apiece.

She signed forms that promised the hospital both her useless arms and legs and tried to be thankful Travis hadn't thrown out her boots with her jacket. She snuck a blanket off a linen cart on her way to the door, but it was still going to be a long, hellish walk home, looking like one of New York's finest. It would be dark soon and was still snowing, growing dusky at three in the afternoon. Her debit card would combust if she so much as tried to put a subway fare on it. She had no choice.

"Bye now," she said as she passed the nurses' station with a wave. "Add this to the bill," she added with a point at the blanket. "Thank you."

"Ms. Gantry," the motherly nurse said in protest. "You really should rest."

"I will," she lied. "Soon as I'm home." She would swing by to see one of her employers on the way, though. See if she still had a job with the biker bar's janitorial staff after blowing her shift last night with this unplanned excursion to the right side of town.

She walked out of the blasting heat in the space between the two sets of automatic doors, and winter slapped her in the face. It immediately sapped 90 percent of her energy, making her sob under her breath as she began putting one foot in front of the other. The cold penetrated before she took ten steps, but she pushed on, doggedly following the looped driveway toward the gilded gates that suggested this place was heaven after all.

It began to look like a really long way just to get to the road. She had to stop and brush snow off a bench dedicated to a hospital benefactor, rest there a moment. She felt so pathetic her eyes began to well. At least her ear didn't hurt like it had. It was just a dull ache.

There was always a bright side if she looked for it.

Nevertheless, panic edged in around the meditative breaths she was blowing like smoke in front of her face. She was shivering, teeth chattering. How was she going to carry on?

One day at a time, she reminded herself, closing her eyes. One footstep at a time.

Before she could rise, a black car stopped at the curb in front of her. The chauffeur came around and opened the back door. She already knew who would get out and tried to pretend she was bored, not so very close to beaten.

Even her father hadn't crushed her as quickly and thoroughly as one irritated look from this man did. He wore a fedora and a gorgeous wool overcoat tailored to his physique. His pants creased sharply down his shins to land neatly on what had to be Italian leather shoes.

"You look like a gangster. I don't have your money. You'll have to break my knees."

"Can those knees get you into this car or do I have to do that for you, too?"

The air was so cold, breathing it to talk made her lungs hurt. "Why do you even care?"

"I don't," he assured her brutally.

She looked back toward the hospital doors. As usual, she'd come too far and had to live with where she had ended up.

"I told the doctor I would get you home if you insisted on leaving and make sure a neighbor checks on you."

The drug dealer across the hall? She would *love* for him to come and go.

She clutched her purse against her chest, inside the blanket she clenched closed with her two hands. She stared at the flakes appearing and melting on her knees so he wouldn't see how close to tears she was.

"I'll find my own way home," she insisted.

Travis, being a man of action, didn't say a word. He swooped so fast she barely had time to realize he had picked her up before he shoved her into the back of his car and followed her in. Abject loss struck before she'd even had time to process the safe feeling of being cradled against his chest.

Dear *God* it was deliciously warm in here. She bit back a moan of relief.

"Now," he said as he slammed his door and sat back, shooting his cuffs. "Where is home, exactly?"

"Didn't the hospital tell you? They seemed so keen to share everything else about me. What is my blood type, anyway? I've never bothered to find out."

He only nodded toward his driver, indicating the man was waiting with more patience than Travis possessed.

They were really doing this? *Fine.* A perverse urge to let him gloat over his pound of flesh gripped her. Maybe if he saw she was being thoroughly punished, he might quit acting so supercilious and resentful.

She stated her address.

The driver's frown was reflected through the rear-view mirror, matching Travis's scowl.

"Would you be serious?" Travis muttered.

She shrugged. "You wanted to know what I was doing in that neighborhood. I live there."

"What are you doing, Imogen?" he asked tiredly. "What's the game? Because I'm not letting you screw me over again."

"No lift home, then?" She put her hand on the door latch.

He sighed. "If I drive you all the way over there, what happens? You get into the bed of some sketchy thug your father didn't approve of?" His lip curled with disgust. His eye twitched, almost as if the idea of it bothered him. "Does he spank you the way you've always needed?"

"Hardly necessary when you're doing such a fine job of that." She glared at him, but holding his gaze was hard. It felt too intimate. They had never played erotic games, but suddenly they were both thinking about it.

While she grew hot, she watched him shut down, locking her out, jaw hardening and a muscle ticking in his cheek.

She swallowed. "I plan to crawl into my own bed and hope I never wake up."

"Tell me where you really live," he said through his teeth.

"I just did." She didn't bother getting emotional about it. It was the doleful truth that her life was so firmly in the toilet, she was barely surviving it.

She let her head rest back and must have dozed, because suddenly he was saying, "We're here," snapping her back to awareness of being in his car.

"Okay. Thanks," she said dumbly, looking behind her to see if it was safe to open her door against traffic.

"You're going through with this, then." Travis swore

beside her and went out his side, then motioned her to come out his side. He had to lean down and help her climb to her feet.

She clung to his hand, shaking, longing to lean into the woolen wall of his chest. Longing to beg, "Don't leave me here." She was scared *all the time*, not that she had the dim sense to show it. It might be a different neighborhood, but the apprehension was the same as she'd always felt in her childhood. Weakness would be pounced upon. She never showed it if she could help it.

She had never been *this* weak, though. It took a superhuman effort to release him from that tenuous connection of grasping his hand—not just physically, but because she felt so lonely. So adrift.

*Why was it so freaking cold out?*

Shivering, she fumbled her key from her purse and moved to the door of her building. It wasn't locked. Never was. The entryway smelled like sauerkraut soup, which was better than some of the other days.

Travis swore as he came in behind her and set a hand on her upper arm, steadying her as she climbed the stairs. His looming presence, intimidating as it was, also felt protective, which made her heart pang.

"Hey," one of her neighbors said as she passed them on the stairs. She was off to work the streets in her thigh-high boots, miniskirt and fringed bra beneath a faux fur jacket. "No tricks in the rooms."

"He's just bringing me home."

"Don't get caught," the woman advised with a shake of her head. "You'll get kicked out."

Imogen didn't look at Travis, but his thunderous silence pulsed over her as she pushed her key into the lock and entered her "home."

It was the room where she slept when she wasn't working but so depressing she would rather work. It was as clean as she could make it, given the communal broom was more of a health hazard than a gritty floor. She didn't have much for personal effects, having sold any clothes and accessories that would bring in a few dollars.

There was a small soup pot on the only chair. It usually held a bag of rice and a box of pasta, but she had dumbly left it in the shared kitchen overnight a few days ago. She was lucky to have recovered the dirty pot. Payday wasn't until tomorrow, which was why she hadn't eaten when she collapsed.

Sinking onto the creaky springs and thin mattress of her low, single bed, she exchanged the damp blanket she'd been clutching around her for the folded one, giving the dry one a weak shake. "Can you leave so they don't think I'm entertaining? I really can't handle being kicked out right now."

"This is where you live." His gaze hit her few other effects: a battered straw basket holding her shampoo, toothbrush and comb, for her trips to the shared bathroom; a towel on the hook behind the door; a windup alarm clock; and a drugstore freebie calendar where she wrote her hours. "The street would be an improvement."

"I tried sleeping on the street. Turns out they call your ex-husband and he shows up to make you feel bad about yourself."

His "Not funny" glare was interrupted by a sharp knock and an even sharper, "No drugs, no tricks! Out!"

"Would you go?" she pleaded.

Travis snapped open the door to scowl at her landlord.

"He's not staying—" she tried to argue, but of course she was on the bed, which looked so very bad.

"We're leaving," Travis said, and snapped his fingers at her.

She flopped onto her side with her back to both of them.

"Imogen."

Oh, she hated her name when it was pronounced like that, as if she was something to be cursed into the next dimension.

"Just *go*," she begged.

"I'm taking this," he said, forcing her to roll over and see he held her red purse.

"Don't." She weakly shook her head. "I can't fight you right now. You know I can't." She was done in. Genuinely ready to break down and cry her eyes out.

"Then you should have stayed in hospital. I'll take you back there now."

She rolled her back to him again. "Take it, then. I don't even care anymore." She really didn't. All she wanted was to close her eyes and forget she existed.

With a string of curses, he dragged the scratchy gray blanket from her and threw it off the foot of the bed. Then he gathered her up, arms so tense beneath the thick wool that her skin felt bruised where it came in contact with his flexed muscles. He was surprisingly gentle in his fury, though, despite cussing out the landlord so he could get by and carry her down the stairs.

"Travis, stop. I'll lose all my things."

"What things? What the hell is going on, Imogen?"

# CHAPTER THREE

IN THE FIVE minutes they'd been upstairs, a handful of jackals had begun circling to case the car. His chauffeur stood ready to open the back door and Travis shoved her into it, wondering why he'd got out at all.

To see how far she would carry her charade, of course, never dreaming she would take him into a dingy firetrap of a room that was where she *actually slept.*

He couldn't even comprehend it.

Snapping a glare at her, he saw there was no fight left in her. Her mouth was pouted, her eyes glassy with exhaustion, her hands limp in her lap.

If she weighed a hundred pounds right now, he'd be stunned. It wasn't healthy, even for a woman barely hitting five and a half feet tall.

"I can't afford the hospital. Can you please just tell my landlord I'm sick, not stoned, and let me sleep?"

"No." He slammed his door and jerked his head at his driver to pull into traffic, wanting away from here. As far and fast as possible. "Do you have gambling debts? What?"

"Oh, I backed the wrong horse. That's for sure." She rolled her head on the back of her seat to quirk her mouth in an approximation of a smile. "What's that old song about not being able to buy love? Turns out it's true."

"Which means?"

She only sighed and closed her eyes, almost as if she was trying to press back tears. "Doesn't matter," she murmured.

"Explain this to me. You had a lover who stole all your money? Tell me, how does that feel?" He ignored the gas-lit inferno that burst into life inside him as he thought of her with other men, feigning great interest in her reply instead.

Her brow pleated and she turned her nose to the front, eyes staying closed. Her lashes might have been damp.

"You seem obsessed with my many lovers. Accuse me of anything, Travis, but not promiscuity. You, of all people, know I don't give it up easily."

That took him aback a little. He didn't understand why. They were divorced. It shouldn't matter to him how many lovers she'd had, so why was he needling her about it? He *presumed* she'd taken some. With her libido?

Sexual memory seared through his blood, lifting the hairs on his body and sending a spike of desire into his loins.

He ignored how thinking of other men enjoying her passionate response put a sick knot in his gut. He had long ago decided he was remembering it wrong, anyway. He'd been high on personal achievements when they'd met, which had lent optimism and ecstasy to their physical encounters. Whatever had been roused in him hadn't been real or wholly connected to her. It certainly hadn't been worth all she'd cost him.

As for what she'd felt?

"Right," he recalled scathingly. "You want a ring and a generous prenup before you sleep with a man. You haven't found another taker for that? Of course, you only have one virginity to barter, and sex without that sweetener?" He hitched a shoulder, dismissing what had felt at the time like an ever-increasing climb of pleasure as she grew more confident with him between the sheets.

His ego needed her to believe his interest had already been waning, though. He still felt embarrassed for going blind with impulsive urgency in the first place, unable to let her get away. He had married her in a rush, on the sly, because he'd known deep down that they wouldn't last. A fire that burned that high, that fast, guttered just as quickly, which was exactly what had happened. A blur of obsessive sex had quickly dissolved into her walking away with her prenuptial settlement and a demand for a divorce.

"Wow," she said, voice husky. "That's hitting below the belt, isn't it? You're welcome, then, for releasing you to enjoy much better sex than I was able to provide."

He wasn't sure how her remark caused his own to bounce back and sting him so deeply. Maybe it was the fact that, try as he might to claim disinterest, he'd never found another woman who'd inspired such a breadth of sexual hunger in him.

That was a good thing, he regularly told himself. Maybe he hadn't erased her from his memory, but he didn't want or need the sort of insanity she had pro-voked, either.

No, he had spent the last years very comfortably dating women who didn't inspire much feeling at all, only returning to the land of turmoil when his PA had interrupted his meeting yesterday morning.

Had it only been thirty-six hours? Such was Imo-gen. She was a hydrogen bomb that cratered a life in seconds, completely reshaping everything around her without a moment's regard.

He remembered her prescription and drew the paper from her purse, handing it to his driver, instructing him to drop them in the front of his building before filling it.

When they arrived at his Chelsea building, how-ever, the doorman was busy corralling paparazzi away from the entrance. It was a common sight when one of his celebrity neighbors had just arrived home. The sidewalks were teeming with Christmas shoppers, too. Even some carolers dressed in olden days' garb.

"Take us to the underground," Travis instructed, be-ginning to feel weary himself. He had only been home for a few hours of sleep last night, arriving late and leaving early, wanting to get back to the hospital. The urgency to do so had been...disturbing. Now he was compelled to get Imogen into his apartment so he could finally relax, which was an equally unsettling impulse.

"You don't want to be photographed with an es-capee from the psych ward? Weird," she murmured. "You realize I don't just *look* like a homeless person? I am one. My landlord will have my stuff on the stoop and my room let to someone else by now. Thanks for that, by the way."

"Still have some spit and vinegar, though."

"Literally, all I have left. Why did you bring me here? Because I'm quite sure you're not inviting me to live with you and I'm quite sure I won't take you up on it if you do."

He didn't know what he was doing, but he hadn't been able to leave her in that roach-infested garbage pail of a building. He imagined she would only discharge herself if he took her back to the hospital. Bringing her to his penthouse was his only choice.

"You're going to have that nap you're so determined to take. I'll use the silence to figure out what to do with you when you wake up."

Imogen wanted to sneer at him, but it took everything in her to open her door when the car stopped and it wasn't even her own steam that did it. The driver got out and opened it for her. He helped her out and Travis came around to slide his arm across her back, helping her into the elevator where he used his fingerprint to override a security panel and take them to the top floor.

He kept his arm around her and she couldn't help but lean into him. It felt really, really nice. For a split second, she experienced a spark of hope. Maybe he didn't hate her. Maybe this was a chance to make amends. She couldn't change the past, but the future was a blank whiteboard.

Then she caught sight of their reflection and her glimmer of optimism died. At one time, she had *almost* been his equal, when her family had had money and she had been a product—not a shining example, but at least a product—of an upper-crust upbringing.

Since then, however, he had skyrocketed from

wealthy architect who dabbled in real estate to international corporate mogul, taking on prestigious projects around the globe. An honest-to-God tycoon who lived in the city's best building on its top floor. He was way out of reach for the black-sheep daughter of a paper publisher and far, far beyond taking up with a match girl—which she could aspire to be as soon as she stole some matches.

She had thought dying in the street was rock bottom. Then Travis seeing how broke she was and the way she had been living had felt like rock bottom. But this was rock bottom. Riding an elevator up to what might have been her life if she'd played her cards differently, while she faced how completely and irrevocably she had fallen down in his estimation, was beyond demoralizing. It was shattering.

Until this moment, her life had been a mess, but her heart had held some resilience. She had possessed some spirit. Some hope that one day she would be able to face him and make amends. That belief had got her out of bed and off to her many awful, minimum-wage jobs. But that was gone now.

The doors of the elevator opened to a foyer of marble and mahogany. Floating stairs rose on the right with a bench tucked beneath. A side table stood on the other side. An impressionist painting the size of Central Park hung above it.

From inside the lounge, out of sight but not out of earshot, Imogen heard an excited voice cry, "Papa!"

As tiny footsteps hurried toward them, Imogen began to disintegrate, each particle of her breaking away and sizzling agonizingly into utter despair.

She was such a fool. *This* was rock bottom.

* * *

Travis bit back a curse as Imogen pulled away from him, swinging a look on him so betrayed and shattered, it cut like a scalpel directly into his heart.

He had to look away to his niece, Antonietta, as she appeared from the lounge. She came up short at the sight of them, recovered in the next second and continued her pell-mell run at him, arms up and wearing a wide smile.

*"Zio!"*

He picked up the three-year-old sprite.

She threw her arms around his neck and made a production of kissing his cheek with a loud, "Mmmwah!"

Gwyn, his stepsister, appeared with a sleeping Enrico drooped on her shoulder. She faltered as she took in that Travis had a woman with him, one who didn't exactly look like his usual type. She wasn't the judgmental sort, though. She quickly recovered with a welcoming smile. "Hi."

"I completely forgot what day it was," Travis told her.

"No problem. I'm Gwyn." She came forward with her free hand extended.

Imogen's gaze sharpened with recognition, but if she said one wrong word to Gwyn...

"You're Travis's sister." Imogen unfolded one arm to shake hands. "Nice to meet you. I'm Imogen."

"Good timing. I've just made coffee," Gwyn said toward Travis. "Let me put Enrico down. I'll be right back."

Imogen's brain was reengaging from its tailspin, where she had briefly been convinced Travis was married with children. She occasionally stalked him online, as one did with an ex. He dated a lot but hadn't seemed serious about anyone, so, for a moment, she had been struck nearly dead with shock. By a loss so acute, she hadn't been able to withstand it.

*Shut up, misguided girlish fantasies.*

She and Travis were *so* over.

As for his sister, when Gwyn had had a spot of trouble a few years ago with an international bank scandal and a global leak of nude photos, Imogen had followed it for different reasons than the rest of the world's lurid curiosity. While she and Travis had been married, he hadn't even *mentioned* he had a stepsister. It had been a shock to see his name associated with the headlines not long after their split. Imogen had combed every story she could find then, trying to figure out why he'd been so secretive about his family.

At the same time, she had drawn a line in the sand for herself. She hadn't told her father that she had an in with that particular story. She and Travis had been firmly on the outs by then, her father's business failing miserably, but she refused to exploit him. Between her divorce settlement and her mother's trust fund, Imogen had been sure they were only a few short months from having her father's company back on its feet.

The core of her reluctance to use Travis, however, had stemmed from the deep agony of rejection Travis's letting her go had rent through her. She hadn't even told her father she'd been married, fearful of his reaction.

He would have approved of Travis, of course, but there was no way she'd wanted Travis to meet her father. Then, when her marriage fell apart...well, who needed that sort of scathing disappointment added to her pain? Her father's derision would have expanded exponentially under the news she had failed to hold on to him. It was bad enough she had deluded herself into believing Travis had had real feelings for her.

The entire thing became so humiliating she had preferred to be as secretive about their marriage as Travis had been.

He led the way into the lounge. It was tastefully decorated for the season with festive garlands around the windows, fairy lights winking in the potted shrubs from the terrace and a tree that looked and smelled real. The presents beneath were professionally wrapped but with cartoonish paper that would appeal to children.

"Mama said I have to ask you if those are for me," the little girl said, one arm still firmly around Travis's neck as she fixed her gaze on the gifts.

"And Enrico, yes."

"Can I open them? *Per favore*, Zio?" she asked very sweetly.

"Not yet."

She gave a little pout of disappointment.

Italian? Imogen sank down on the sofa so she wouldn't fall down.

"You never mentioned your sister," she commented. All he'd told her was that he was close with his father, who lived in Charleston, and didn't see much of his mother, but she also lived in that city.

"Gwyn's mother married my father while I was at university, but passed away soon after. Gwyn and I didn't grow up together."

They seemed close now, if he was giving the woman access to his apartment when he wasn't even here. He'd been cautious about letting his *wife* into his personal space, constantly picking up behind her and uptight that the few things she'd brought with her hadn't fit with his existing decor. At the time, she had put it down to the shift from bachelorhood to living with someone, but she knew now it had been more than a territorial thing. He hadn't wanted her there at all. It still made her throat raw to think of it.

"This is Antonietta." He was still holding her. "We call her Toni."

The little girl cupped her hand near his ear and whispered something.

The corner of his mouth twitched. "Toni Baloney."

Toni giggled and hunched her shoulders up to her ears. "What's your name?"

"Imogen. My sister used to call me Imogen the Imagination Magician."

Toni widened her eyes in excited wonder. "I love that name."

He didn't just have family, but a fun and loving one. Huh. Why would he have felt a need to hide that from her?

"Come eat your apples and cheese, *topolina*," Gwyn said as she returned, waving Toni toward the snack at the elegant glass-topped pedestal dining table.

Travis set the girl on her feet and she skipped across to climb up and kneel on a velvet-upholstered chair.

Imogen hadn't been allowed at the grown-up table until she was twelve.

"The doorman let us up because you left notice that we would arrive today." Gwyn came over with coffee, cream and sugar, then seated herself where she could watch Toni. "I thought that meant you remembered we were coming. I was going to text, but I got busy with the kids. If we're imposing, I'll ask Vito to move us to a hotel."

"It's one night. I forgot, that's all." Travis seemed to blame Imogen for his absentmindedness with the cool glance he flicked her way as he sat.

Imogen lifted her brows, wondering how he was going to explain her presence now that his worlds had collided.

He didn't bother, only sat back with his black coffee. "Vito had meetings?"

After a beat of surprise, Gwyn nodded. She smiled at Imogen. "We just got in from Italy. My husband often has business in New York, so we make a stop here, adjust to the jet lag, let the kids leave fingerprints all over Zio's furniture, then head to Charleston."

"To see Travis's father?"

"Henry, yes. And the bank has offices there. Vito checks in and works on and off while we visit Nonno. For the last few years, Henry has been coming to us for the holidays, but this year is his seventieth birthday. It's right before Christmas and he's having a party, so we came to him."

"Sounds fun." Imogen deliberately offered nothing about herself.

"It should be."

Silence reigned as they all blew across coffee that was too hot to drink.

The corners of Gwyn's mouth wore the tiniest curl. She was clearly dying to pry, but was far too polite to ask. Or knew Travis would talk when he was ready and not before. Imogen had come up against that perversely closed-off side of him herself. In fact, the things

Gwyn had just told her were probably the most she'd
ever learned about his personal life.

"Toni, do you see an elephant in this room?" Imogen turned her head to ask.

Gwyn snorted and almost spilled her coffee.

Toni sat up on her knees and swung her head this
way and that. "No."

"Mmm... My mistake. I thought there was one."

Travis sent her a warning look.

"We've taken up both guest rooms, but the kids can
come into our room if need be," Gwyn said mildly.

"Is there an aquarium?" Imogen asked Toni. "Because I feel like someone is fishing."

Gwyn had to scratch her nose to hide the laugh she
suppressed.

Toni cocked her head, sensing opportunity. "We can
pretend to fish in the pool."

"It's too cold, *topolina*," Gwyn said. "When Papa
gets back and Enrico is awake, we could maybe go
to the indoor one downstairs. You and I are going to
have a little sleep first, though. Soon as you finish
your snack."

"And Imogen?"

Imogen plucked at the pajamas she was wearing,
certain that was what had prompted Toni's question.
"I'm going to nap, too, but by myself."

Travis looked at Gwyn. "Would you have something
that Imogen could wear when she wakes?"

"Of course. I'll find something right now."

Gwyn took Toni upstairs and Travis finished his coffee,
watching Imogen while wishing for something stronger in his cup. He knew he should check his phone.

He'd been ignoring it since walking out of that meeting yesterday. Finding Gwyn here reminded him he had a life beyond Imogen. A trip to Charleston in a few days for his father's birthday and the family Christmas celebrations.

He couldn't think of anything, however, except the woman who had had a way of consuming his thoughts from the moment he'd met her. She had walked into his brand-new offices here in New York four years ago, as he'd been expanding beyond Charleston, starting some of his most prestigious architectural projects to date.

She'd introduced herself as a writer for one of the cornerstone publications in New York and proceeded to interview him. Her auburn hair had rippled in satin waves as she'd canted her head at him, listening in a way that had made him feel ten feet tall.

"Let's talk more over dinner," he had suggested after an hour of growing ever more fascinated by her engaging curiosity and earnest little frowns. Her legs were lithe stems beneath a black miniskirt, propping up a notebook where her handwriting looped in big swirls and *t*'s that she crossed with a sweep of her slender wrist. Her breasts had looked to be the exact fit for his palms. Everything about her had looked like a perfect fit. She had been, not that he had had confirmation that first night. Dinner had turned into an invitation back to his old apartment, which was when she had confessed to being a virgin.

"At twenty?" he'd chided with skepticism. "How is that possible?"

"Probably because I don't know what I'm missing," she had shot back, laughing at herself yet surprising him into laughing, as well.

That quick wit, that unvarnished honesty, had convinced him she was exactly what she appeared—a journalism student from a good family with a bright mind and a cheeky wit that would keep him on his toes. There was absolutely nothing to dislike in that package.

The packaging had been the lie, of course. Mislabeled. Ingredients not as advertised. Definitely looking shopworn these days.

Finishing her coffee, she set down her cup, bringing him back to the present.

"You don't want me here. I'll go." She looked around, frowning. She was probably looking for her purse, which was in the pocket of his overcoat. He'd hung it in the closet at the door. It could stay there for now.

"Where to?" he prompted. Goaded. He was fed up with her thinking she had options when clearly neither of them did.

She swallowed. "I'll talk to my landlord—"

"No," he cut in.

She turned a look on him that sparked with temper. "What do you want from me, Travis?"

"Let's start with an explanation. Where did all my money go?" He waved at the fact her worldly possessions consisted of pajamas she hadn't been able to pay for out of her own pocket. "Where did *yours* go?" She hadn't been rich, but she hadn't been destitute.

She blew out a breath and sagged into the sofa, pulling a tasseled cushion into her middle.

He braced, waiting to see if she would tell the truth or lie yet again. Wondering if he would be able to tell the difference.

"I was trying to save Dad's business."

"Publishing," he recalled.

"Newspapers and magazines." She gave him a pained smile. "Print media."

He recalled what she'd said in the car. "'The wrong horse.'"

"Such a dead one, yet I beat it like you can't even imagine. Your money, my trust fund. Dad sold the house and liquidated anything that wasn't already in the business. We threw every penny we had at it. Then he went into care, which was another bunch of bills. My name wound up on everything. I couldn't declare bankruptcy while he was alive. It was too humiliating for him. We were pretending it was all systems go while I sold furniture and clothes and Mom's jewelry to make ends meet. His cremation was the final straw. I was behind on rent and got evicted. I wasn't really keeping up on friendships by then and owed money to the few friends I had left. I wanted to start over on my own terms, so I found something I could afford and that's what I'm doing."

"That roach-infested brothel is your idea of a fresh start? Why didn't you come to me?"

"Oh, that's funny," she said with an askance look. "What would you have said?"

Everything he was saying now, but he wouldn't have let her get to where she was passing out on the street from neglecting her health.

"You married me to get your hands on your trust fund. Didn't you?" She had never admitted it, but he was convinced of it.

She hesitated very briefly before nodding, eyes downcast. Guilt? Or hiding something?

"I wanted access to it so I could help Dad." She had

the humility to shake her head and quirk her mouth in self-contempt. "Not exactly an economist over here. I knew better. Digital publishing was all I learned at school, which he thought was useless." She shrugged. "I tried to convince him to start doing things online, but old dogs…" She smiled without humor. "It would have been too little, too late, even if he'd bought in."

"So, you're broke."

"I'm in a hole so deep all I see is stars."

"You're telling me the truth? Because if it's addiction or something, tell me. I'll get you help."

"I wish it was. There would be pain relief, at least. Escape." Her smile was a humorless flat line.

He drummed his fingers on the arm of his chair, frustrated by what sounded like brutal honesty. Nevertheless, he muttered, "God, I wish I could trust you."

"What does it matter if you do or don't? I mean, thanks for the hospital, I guess. I'll try to pay you back someday, when I can afford a lottery ticket and happen to win the jackpot, but—" she flicked a helpless hand in the air "—our lives won't intersect after today, so…"

Her heart lurched as she said those words, trying to be laissez-faire about it.

He narrowed his eyes. "That would be nice if it were true, but I've just taken responsibility for your hospital bills. For *you*. What am I going to do? Turn you out on the street? In the middle of winter? I happen to possess a conscience."

"Meaning I don't?"

"It was pretty damned calculating, what you did."

"You're the one who set the terms of the prenup,"

she reminded him. "That was all you. All I did was sign it."

"And took the money after three weeks of marriage."

"Oh, I should have given you my virginity for the bragging rights of saying I was once Travis Sanders's lay of the day?" She blinked her lashes at him, pretending her shields were firmly in place when she was silently begging him to contradict her. To say she had meant more to him than that.

She *had* been willing to give it up without a ring in the heat of passion, if he would only remember. He was the one who had proposed and led her to believe he cared.

A muscle pulsed in his jaw. "I'm surprised you haven't sold our story, if you needed money so badly."

She pressed her lips together, but he was quick enough to read her expression.

"Considered it, did you? I cannot believe I thought we had a shot," he muttered.

"Oh, did you?" She leaped on that. "Did you really? How about you step off your high horse a minute and be honest about your own motives. Why did *you* marry *me*?"

"You know why. You refused to sleep with me until I put a ring on it."

"And you wanted in my pants so bad, you wanted bragging rights to my virginity so bad, you made our quickie marriage happen." They'd known each other a *week*. "Then what? Did you take me home to meet this wonderful family of yours, all flushed with pride in your darling bride? You didn't even tell me you had a sister." She thumbed toward the stairs. "She hasn't got a clue who I am. Does your dad?"

His stony expression told her that was a hard no.

"At no point did you think we had a shot." The words were coming out thick and scathing, but they tore up her insides, sharp as barbed wire, seeming to affect her far more than him. "You were mortified that you'd succumbed to marriage. Every time I said, 'Let's go out,' you said, 'Let's stay in.' The one time we ran into someone you knew, you didn't even introduce me. You didn't just skip the part that I was your wife. You didn't acknowledge me to them *at all*."

His cheek ticked and he looked away, not offering an explanation, which scored another fresh line down her heart.

"You wouldn't let me change my status online and said it was because you wanted me to yourself. Then you went to work every day, leaving me alone in that big apartment where I wasn't allowed to touch anything."

"You claimed to be writing for your father, if I recall. Why did I never see any of those articles?" So scathing.

Her face stung, but she wasn't about to get into her father's lack of love for her. One spurn was all she could relive at a time, thanks.

"You were planning our divorce before you said, 'I do.' That's why you drew up the prenup. All you cared about was keeping the damage to your reputation at a minimum. You invested *nothing* in our relationship except what I took when I left, certainly not your heart. Our marriage was as much a transaction on your side as mine. I bruised your *ego* by walking out before you told me to leave, not your feelings. Tell me I'm wrong."

*Please.* She silently begged him to give her a rosier view of their flash-in-the-pan romance. Her whole body tingled, ions reaching out for a positive against this negative charge consuming her.

"Fine," he bit out. "You're right. I knew it was a mistake even as I was saying the words."

His words skewered into her. She swallowed, wishing she had died in the gutter, rather than survive to face this.

"You're welcome for remaining your dirty little secret, then," she snapped. "For what it's worth, you're one of thousands of mistakes I've made. Not unique or special at all."

"You don't know when to quit, do you?" he said in a dangerous voice. "Aside from the day you walked out, of course."

"Oh, you started that. You know you did."

"A husband is allowed to ask his wife why he needs to top up her credit card before it's a month old," he said through his teeth.

"Your exact words were, 'I don't care where it went.' You didn't want to know about my life any more than you wanted to share details about yours. I quit kidding myself at that point. It wasn't a marriage if you were suffering buyer's remorse. I did you a favor by walking out."

"That's one way to frame it."

"Yeah, well, I keep trying to do you the favor of walking away again, but you keep forcing me to sit my butt back down. Why is that?"

"Because you owe me, Imogen." He leaned forward,

hand gripping the arm of his chair as though trying to keep himself in it.

"I owe a lot of people. Get in line."

The sound of the elevator had them both holding their stare but clamming up while the animosity cracked and bounced between them.

A superbly handsome man appeared in a bespoke suit. Little sparkles came off him where snowflakes had melted across his shoulders and in his dark hair. He was clean-shaven, calm and confident, not taken aback in the least by the sight of an orphan in hospital pajamas huddling on Travis's designer sofa.

"You must be Imogen," he said with a heart-melting Italian accent, coming forward to take her hand in a gentlemanly shake. "No, don't get up. Vittorio Donatelli. Vito, *per favore*."

"Gwyn texted you?" Travis surmised.

"And the photographers downstairs inform me that Imogen is your wife. *Congratulazioni*," he said to Travis with a blithe smile. "They asked for a comment. I told them I'm very happy for you, of course."

"Are you kidding?" Travis closed his eyes and Imogen was pretty sure steam came out his ears.

"I didn't say a word," she swore.

"You didn't have to, did you?"

"My passport lapsed! My student card was long gone. Sometimes you need more than one piece of ID. Why would anyone give a care who I was married to? I'm nobody and you're just one more businessman in a city of—" She cut herself off as she saw a look pass between the men.

Gwyn, she remembered. Travis's sister was notorious clickbait.

"It's not her fault," Travis said to Vito.

"I will assure her of that, but you know what she's like." Vito's smile was pained as he rubbed the back of his neck and excused himself to go upstairs.

"For what it's worth, that's one of the reasons I never told a soul you and I were married," Imogen said. "Once I saw what the online trolls were doing to her, I not only didn't want to be part of it, but I had enough people willing to pile on me. It would have only made things worse for her to be associated in this direction."

He stared at her. "You really want me to believe you were thinking of her?"

And him, but what was the use in trying to convince him? "You either believe me or you don't, Travis. I can't make you do anything."

It hurt to acknowledge his mistrust. All of this was even more excruciating than being one more anonymous hard-luck story in a building full of society's rejects.

"It's actually your fault that our marriage has been exposed, you know," she pointed out. "Some orderly probably saw you acting like a big shot, transferring your wife to Celebrity Central. You in your tailored suit, flashing your gold-plated phone. You should have left me at the first hospital and none of this would be happening."

He picked up his phone and said, "It's last year's model. Off the shelf."

"Whatever. You made me look important. I wasn't trying to be."

"Let's skip the blame shifting and get to mitigating the damage. You really owe me now." He tapped and rolled the phone along its edge on the arm of his chair, thoughts hidden behind an expression gone granite hard. "This is going to be all over the gossip sites. Maybe the financial pages and television news outlets. I imagine they'll dig up the date of our marriage and the divorce settlement."

As much as she had rationalized taking that settlement, she had always felt ashamed of herself for demanding it.

He had been contemptuous in fulfilling it, making clear that whatever physical infatuation he'd felt toward her had firmly run its course. She repulsed him on every level.

She had dreamed ever since of paying him back, just to soften his harsh opinion of her, but she knew from her childhood what a lost cause that sort of aspiration was.

"It won't be long before my father is calling me, asking whether this report of my marriage is true."

"What do you want me to do?" She held up her powerless hands.

"I'll tell you what I want you to do. *Don't humiliate me again.*"

Was that what she had done? Because when she had been standing there, wanting to make explanations about her father's business and how painful her relationship was with him, she'd felt pretty damned humiliated to realize Travis didn't care one iota that she had reasons and responsibilities and that she suffered. He had decided she was a faithless spendthrift well before she'd returned from her father's office that day.

"This is what you're going to do," he said in a voice so hard it couldn't be scratched. "You're going to say our marriage was youthful impulse and we parted ways when we realized our mistake. After your father passed, you began doing charity work, which is how you happened to be on skid row when you needed medical attention. I'll make suitable donations to back that up. Then we're going to show the world that we might have parted over artistic differences, but I had the taste and sense to marry very well. You're going to stay with me, pretend we're reconciling and act like the kind of wife you should have been."

*Bad girl. I didn't say you could come out of your room. Get back up there.*

She swallowed back the bitter pill in the back of her throat. "Is that what I'm going to do?"

"Unless you're ready to start making a living the way your neighbor appeared to earn hers, you are going to do exactly what I tell you to do."

"You don't see the irony of introducing me to your friends and family now, when I'm not actually married to you, when you were ashamed to call me your wife before?"

"It galls me," he assured her, leaning back and catching at his pant leg as he crossed one over the other, flinty expression belying his relaxed pose. "But the cat is out of the bag. We're going to groom it and put a pretty collar on it and keep it from scratching up the furniture."

"And somehow this pays off my debt to you."

"It keeps it from getting worse."

Oh, she doubted that.

The walls were closing in another inch. They'd been compressing on her for months. Years, even. No options. It was a trapped, helpless feeling and she could only sit there with her hands knotted into fists and breathe.

"You don't have anywhere to go," he pointed out, as if she wasn't sickeningly aware. "How do I look if I put you on the street? No, we're rediscovering each other. At *Christmas*. It's very romantic," he said with thick sarcasm. "The press will be very positive."

He said the last in a way that was more of a threat. *Mind yourself, Imogen, or you'll stay in your room.*

"How long will this last?"

"Until I feel the attention has died down enough we can part without it being noteworthy."

"But I'll still owe you for the hospital bills." She flicked nonexistent lint from her pajama pants. "Too bad you won't have sex with me. Otherwise, I could pay that down *exactly* the way my neighbor does."

"I didn't say I wouldn't sleep with you. I said you need to work harder to make it interesting."

For a moment, all she heard was a rush in her ears. Her face grew hot. She wanted to believe it was anger, but it was embarrassment. Acute insecurity. No matter what she did or how hard she tried, she was never enough. It was a hot coal of humiliation that burned a hole in her belly every single day.

"Well." She clung fiercely to what shredded dignity she had left, but she was dying inside. "I've only had one lover and he taught me all I know, so blame yourself. But after that remark, I'd rather give it away to strangers on the street than sleep with you again." She stood.

He shot to his feet, arm jerking as though he would stop her in her tracks.

She wasn't walking out, though. As he had pointed out so ruthlessly, she had nowhere to go.

She tucked her elbows into her sides, avoiding his touch. "Powder room?"

He gave a brief nod toward the far end of the kitchen.

She locked herself inside, then splashed cold water onto her burning eyes.

# CHAPTER FOUR

TRAVIS TOOK ZERO satisfaction in having pierced her shell. There had been such hurt in her for a moment, the kind of betrayed shock that came after a sucker punch, he had thought she was walking out on him and his heart had lurched. He'd been ready to physically stop her.

Even though letting her go would be the healthier choice for both of them. He *was* hitting below the belt, but there'd been something in her flippant remark about paying him off with sex that had struck a raw spot. Her accusation of his treating their marriage like a transaction and having buyer's remorse was stuck in his craw, too.

Was that how he had viewed it?

He certainly hadn't looked on marriage as a sacred vow. His parents had divorced. It was something people did. That had allowed him to see a viable exit strategy even as he was proposing. She wasn't wrong about that.

*I bruised your ego by walking out before you told me to leave.*

He hadn't been ready, that was true. He had still wanted her—still did, if the way his blood had leaped at her talk of trading sex was anything to go by. Cop-ping to that would give her the upper hand, though, and she already had too much of his attention.

One lover? Really? *Impossible.*

She had said earlier she wasn't promiscuous. Okay, he was willing to believe she was fastidious, but to want him to believe she'd only been with *him*? Lying about that was worse than all the rest, almost as if she knew it was his Achilles' heel.

He couldn't let himself believe anything she said, but in all their sparring today, nothing had landed so hard on him as the way she kept insisting she hadn't been with other men. If it was actually true—

It couldn't be. It would leave him reeling. And she had overturned his life enough.

His phone rang, vibrating through his hard grip when he'd forgotten he was even holding it. It was his father. The rumors had reached him via a friend who'd seen something online. Travis promised to explain once they were in Charleston. No escape from this charade now.

The reality of pretending to be enamored with his ex-wife began to hit him. Better to manage the PR with her under his nose, however, than let her loose to ruin herself, maybe even him, all over again.

*One lover.*

Why did he want to believe that so badly?

The elevator pinged as his driver delivered her medication. Gwyn came down the stairs as he accepted it and followed him back to the kitchen.

"I shouldn't have had the coffee," Gwyn said with a yawn. "Vito is fast asleep, but I'm wide awake so thought I'd start dinner. I left a dress for Imogen in your room. Is she still here?"

"In the powder room." He glanced down the hall, heard the water running. He moved to check her prescription and shook out a couple of pills to give her when she came out.

"Is she staying for dinner?"

"Yes."

"Did you talk to Henry?" Gwyn pulled vegetables from the fridge.

"Yes."

She paused to send him an exasperated look. "You were so angry with me for not speaking up when everything was happening with the bank. You know I want to help if you need something, right?"

"Cooking dinner is always appreciated."

She rolled her eyes, moving around his kitchen with familiarity.

This was one of the reasons he invited them to sleep here instead of a hotel. She provided some of the only home-cooked meals he ever ate.

Imogen had been a good cook, he recalled. That had been why he preferred to stay in. That and who wanted to get dressed again after sex? Today was probably the first time since they'd married that he had walked into an apartment with her and not stripped them naked in a matter of seconds.

Gwyn started garlic sizzling along with basil and oregano, saying, "We could stay an extra day. I could take her shopping if you like."

He had been suspicious of Gwyn and her mother when his father had moved them into his home. He'd since learned that beneath Gwyn's stunning exterior was a heart of pure gold. Her longing for family ran so deep, and her determination to stitch one together was so dogged, she had somehow pressed him into forming ties with her husband and children. He had enormous affection for her.

Which was why he didn't want her to get hurt.

"Don't get attached," he said in gentle warning. "This is damage control. It's not going to last."

Her optimistic expression fell into concerned lines. "But I want this for you."

He shrugged off her picture-perfect life. "I was never cut out for marriage and kids."

She dismissed that with a snort. "Vito would have said the same thing four years ago. *We* started as damage control."

"Vito didn't know what he was dealing with. Imogen doesn't possess your lovable nature."

Gwyn flushed and grinned at the compliment, but her smile fell away into embarrassed regret as she looked past him.

He turned to see Imogen had emerged from the hallway, expression stiff after hearing what he'd just said.

*I can't do this*, Imogen thought as she put on the sweater dress Gwyn had left for her. It hung off her like a sack.

It wasn't just how frumpy she looked. It was symbolic of how she didn't fit into Travis's world *at all*.

She had spent virtually her whole life trying to belong where she didn't. An interloper in her own family, the wrong crowd of friends, her father's choice of degree and a husband ashamed of their marriage. She couldn't go downstairs to eat with his family and pretend she was a *good wife*. One with a *heart*.

She was so very *dis*heartened by all of this that she pushed the dress off her shoulders so it fell to the floor, then crawled into the bed. Travis's bed. She honestly didn't care what he would think of her being so proprietary. What was he going to do? See it as a boring, extremely unimaginative attempt at seduction and revile her for it?

*No need to sing another chorus of that, husband darling.*

Curling into a ball, she brought the blankets up to her chin and fought tears as she tried to think. She had to figure out how to get back on her feet. Pull up her socks. Put things back to rights so she could get out of here, but it was all so horribly uphill.

She honestly didn't think she was that bad a person, just someone who had made some really dumb mistakes out of blind optimism. That wasn't the sort of character flaw that should leave her in such a ditch. It seemed really unfair.

It shouldn't be this hard to...

...sneak into Juliana's room.

She was so *hungry*. Her belly growled like a monster, but Daddy had locked her door, swearing really loud and angry, telling her to stay there this time. But she wanted out. She wanted to ask Juliana to bring her some bread. Or braid her hair. That always made her feel better. She was so sad. So lonely. All she had done was run up the stairs. She knew she wasn't supposed to run in the house, but he had told her to hurry and she had forgotten her hair band. He hated when her hair fell onto her face. Said it made her look like a stray.

Mama was saying things downstairs, making him shout even more. Mama's voice was soft, like she was crying, but Daddy's voice came through the floor like thunder, shaking Imogen's bed: "I told you!" and "Never should have had her."

He didn't want her and she didn't know why. The tears she'd been holding back began to seep through her closed eyes to wet her lashes. She couldn't help it. She pushed her face into the pillow so he wouldn't hear her sob. If he came to the door and heard her crying, she had to stay in longer. She could only come out if she was *good*.

*Please come, Juliana. Please.*

Like a miracle, the mattress shifted next to her. A soft "Shh" sounded near her ear as warm arms engulfed her. But these arms weren't her sister's soft, skinny arms. They were hot, muscled arms that enveloped her in a way that felt even safer.

"Travis," she whispered.

For a moment, she thought she was waking from a different bad dream. One where she and Travis had had an awful fight and she'd gone back to her father. They were still married after all. His skin branded her torso and thighs as she slithered close and melted against him, deeply relieved and instantly growing sensual, wanting to feel his body with all of hers. He smelled amazing and made her feel so cherished. His hand caressed down her spine, stirring her blood.

He was aroused, all of him stiffening as she slid her hand down his abdomen.

His muscles tensed and his hands shifted to press her away. "Don't."

Reality crashed onto her like an anvil dropping onto a hapless cartoon character.

With an anguished, mortified gasp, she rolled away and fought out of the tangled blankets. Her eyes released a fresh sheen of tears, frustrated, angry ones that choked up her chest and made her whole body shudder in confused reaction. She was half aroused, half traumatized by the betrayal of waking up *into* a nightmare.

Throwing her legs off the edge of the bed, she sat up, head pounding with a sudden rush of blood. She cradled her skull in two hands, elbows digging into her thighs, and consciously dragged her breaths into a slower cadence, grappling to face harsh reality all over again.

She was grown up and not even the married Imogen. She was the divorced, abandoned, impoverished one.

"You still have those?" He touched her back. "You're shaking."

She shrugged him off and used the edge of the sheet to wipe her cheeks. Then she used her forearm to hide her breasts in the dark while she stood and searched through the shadows for her hospital clothes.

"Where are you going?"

"I'm hungry." It was true, but she needed away from him so she could regroup. The dream had only happened a couple of times while they'd been married, but he had held her and stroked her then, soothing her and making love to her, encouraging her to bond with him in ways she couldn't risk again.

Not that he was offering, practically pushing her away like she was toxic.

This arrangement was going to be excruciating.

She hurriedly dressed and he followed her downstairs wearing jeans and nothing else. She averted her eyes from the smooth planes of his chest, the dark stubble coming in on his jaw.

The light over the stove was on, casting the kitchen in a soft glow. As she took yogurt from the fridge, he brought a box of muesli out of the pantry.

She sprinkled some over the yogurt in the bowl and took it to the table.

He brought over a glass of water and a capsule from her prescription. She'd had one before going upstairs to change, but had fallen asleep and missed the one she should have taken after dinner.

"Do you want toast? I can warm the leftovers."

"This is fine."

He touched the backs of his fingers to her cheek.

She pulled away, emotions so raw, even a gentle caress against her skin was liable to bruise all the way to her soul.

"I'm checking for fever."

"I'm fine." She lifted her hair off her neck where it was still damp with sweat from her dream.

He stayed beside her, fingertips going into his front pockets. "I suppose you still won't tell me what those are about?"

"They're just something I fake to earn your sympathy. Don't fall for it."

He swore under his breath, walking away then, standing to look out on the covered pool, blanketed with snow. His silhouette was heartbreakingly strong and beautiful against the glow.

His voice was marginally less confrontational as he asked, "Have you ever talked to anyone about them?"

"Why?"

"So they might stop."

"I'll sleep down here so I don't wake you."

"That's not the point." He swung around. "You

sound like you're in pain. You wake up with your heart pounding. You can't enjoy that."

She only took another bite and chewed, making herself swallow.

"Maybe if you talked about it, your mind wouldn't create monsters while you sleep."

"It's a memory."

A beat of surprise, then he asked very carefully, "Of a monster?"

"I wasn't molested. Don't freak out." She tipped the bowl and scraped yogurt toward the bottom side. "It's a replay of a no-good, rotten day when I was a kid." One of many, actually. "But sometimes, if I don't wake up right away, Juliana comes to visit me. So it's worth it to me to let it happen."

"Juliana is your sister?" He sounded almost gentle. "The one who passed away?"

"Yes."

"Why didn't you tell me that before?"

"Because I didn't want to." She chased the last bite and ate it. "I liked when you felt sorry for me and snuggled me. It felt nice. And I was afraid you might go to my father about it if I told you."

"Why?"

She threw her pill into her mouth and drank all the water, discovering she was super thirsty. She took her dirty dishes to the sink and poured herself more water, turning to lean against the sink and gaze across the miles of space between them.

Dare she pry open the darkest closet in her heart and show him the ugliest skeleton? Her dignity was long gone and that was all she had ever wanted to protect. Her father wasn't here to make it worse.

"Keep in mind I was twenty when you and I married. I've grown up a lot since then. I've had four years to realize Dad was the wrong horse to give a rat's behind about, but back then, I was still holding out hope I had a chance with him. I wasn't ready to cut the pulsating, infected cord that bound me to him."

"What kind of chance?" She couldn't see his frown, but she heard it in his voice.

"That he would love me." She took a sip to clear the constriction that began to squeeze her throat as she said it aloud for the first time. She had always known it, but now it was real. Acknowledged. *Fact*.

"Imogen—" his tone said, "Silly girl" "—lots of teenagers fall out with their parents."

"He hated me, Travis. *Hated* me."

"Why?" He still had that overly patient cast to his voice, like she was being dramatic or something.

"Ask him," she suggested with a scrape of humorless laughter in her throat. "I asked him once if my mother had had an affair. I thought maybe I was some other man's kid and that's why he couldn't accept me. He said, no, he just didn't want me."

"He said that? Those words? To your face?"

"He did. My parents' marriage was a business merger and he only agreed to Mom having Juliana because he needed an heir, but he didn't want another one. Mom wanted Juliana to have a sibling and wanted another baby for herself. She even tried the argument about an heir and a spare. He said no, but she stopped her pills and got pregnant anyway. He had taken to my sister. Mom thought he would warm up to me once I arrived. He didn't. I think hating me so openly was his way of punishing her for going against his wishes."

"This is the father you spent all my money bailing out?"

"You're entitled to your outrage." She tried pouring more water on the fire in her throat, but it stayed scorched and agonized. "I'm sure Mom is rotating like a rotisserie chicken in her grave over it."

"Why would you—?"

"Try to make my father love me? Because I was his child. He should have loved me. Isn't that the way it's supposed to work? But he didn't. Why, I don't know. Why didn't *you* love me? Because I'm bad? *Unlovable?*"

"Imogen." He said it like an imprecation and his hand came up.

"Don't feel bad about saying that." She waved off any nudge of conscience he might be experiencing over what she'd heard him say to Gwyn. "Maybe I'm not lovable. If so, it's his DNA that did that to me. He didn't know how to be anything better than he was and neither do I. I *tried* to be like Juliana. She was so good and sweet. He loved her. Everyone did. I did. You would have."

She looked for more to eat in the refrigerator. Some of Toni's leftover apple and cheese sat on a plate with plastic wrap. She took that out and looked for the bread.

"Was he an alcoholic or something?"

"No, just a bitter, cruel bastard. He used to lock me in my room without dinner to get me out of his sight. If I talked too loud or had raindrops on my clothes or got a better mark in spelling than Juliana, he would point at the stairs."

She carefully arranged the cheese and apples on one slice of bread, eating the chunk that didn't fit.

"I was smarter than her. A lot smarter. She struggled to read and sometimes I did her homework for her. I think that was part of his animosity. He liked being superior to everyone around him. I was always coming back with a joke or asking for more information. If he didn't know the answer or I got a laugh, he thought I was trying to make him look stupid."

"You should have told me."

"Why? What would you have done? Told him to love me? I knew when Mom and Juliana died that it was a lost cause. I just wasn't ready to admit it."

She pushed the heel of her hand down on the sandwich so it was thin as paper and about as appetizing. Her heart felt equally mashed to nothing. A nauseating ache had sat in her chest her whole life as she'd tried to figure out why she was such a disappointment.

"Want to know what he said that day, after the police came to the house?"

"Probably not," he said, grim and low.

She concentrated on cutting the crusts from her sandwich so she wouldn't have to lift her gaze. She was so ashamed of the memory, still so utterly devastated, that she didn't know where she got the courage to recollect it, but it was part of this ghost that needed exorcism.

"He was already angry. He had had to pick me up from my dance lesson because Mom didn't show up. She had slid off the road, into the river with Juliana. The police found them hours later. I was supposed to be in my room, of course, but when I heard someone at the door, I snuck out to see if it was them. I was at the top of the stairs as they explained what happened. Dad thanked them and closed the door. When he saw me, he said, 'The runt is the one who is supposed to drown.'"

"Is that *true*?" Travis's fists were so tight she could see the bulge of veins in his forearms all the way from over here.

"That was his reaction," she said, voice scraped raw by the past. "I couldn't even process that I had lost my mother and sister, but all he said was 'Go to your room.' Then he locked himself in his study until the funeral."

She had needed Juliana so badly then, but all she'd had was one hug from a housekeeper who had helped her find something to wear.

"I was eleven, just young enough to believe if I tried hard enough, he would change and learn to care about me, since I was all he had left. I worked really hard at school, hung around with all the spoiled preppy kids who came from families he admired. I didn't find one person I had a single thing in common with, but I *tried*. I took a degree in journalism, even though I was more of a fiction person. All the profs said my work was too purple. I wrote for Dad's dying rags, even though he only assigned me fluff pieces and only published my work if he absolutely had to. You thought I interviewed you as bait, trying to con you into our marriage, but I saw what an up-and-comer you were. My article was actually really good, but he cut it at the last minute. I tried to sell it to his competitor for you, because it was good press. We had a huge fight about it. We fought a lot and I always stormed out, saying awful things, but I always crawled back. They say the definition of *crazy* is to keep doing the same thing expecting a different result. I'm certifiable."

She ate her crusts out of habit. She cut them off

because she didn't like them, but knew better than to waste food, so she always got rid of them first.

"I was feeling pretty full of myself when we married. I almost quit and walked out of his house for good. I didn't need him if I had you, right? Then I realized you didn't actually care for me, that you only married me for my virginity. Seemed better to go back to the devil I knew, then. At least I had something he wanted. Maybe I could save his company and finally earn his respect."

She didn't know if he was even breathing. He stood so still, he could have been carved from marble. It made it easier to talk around the drill bit hollowing out her chest, leaving curled shards of her soul on the floor. She was confessing her sins to a statue, not a real person. It was a relief to finally get it all out.

"In the end, he hated me even more than you do, because I saw him at his weakest. I spent a solid year looking after him until I just couldn't do it anymore. Physically. He was too heavy for me to get into the bath. I had to put him into care. He hated me for that, too. I shouldn't have been born, I wasn't his favorite, I didn't save his business and I abandoned him to strangers—even though I spent hours every day with him at the home, fetching anything his nonexistent heart desired. I don't know why he was such a twisted, awful person. I'm sorry I was born to him, too. And embarrassed. That's why I never told you. I mean, who wants to admit her own father didn't love her?"

She picked up the sandwich, knowing she needed to eat it but feeling quite sick now, not sure she could swallow a single bite.

"Whenever I go to bed hungry and feeling sorry for

myself, I dream I'm locked in my bedroom again. If she can, Juliana sneaks in to make me feel better. You're the only person it's ever bothered because you're the only person I've ever slept next to. But I don't expect you to believe any of this. I'm a bad apple who never should have been born."

She bit into her sandwich and forced her jaw to chew.

The crying in her sleep was real. That much he knew. She sounded like a child when she was in the throes of her dream and came awake so shaken and confused, there was no way she was faking it.

He remembered the first time her tears had woken him, just a few days after he'd moved her into his old apartment. They'd had a fight earlier that evening about whether to tell anyone they were married. Rather than take her out for dinner, they'd had makeup sex until they fell asleep, utterly exhausted. He had thought she was crying about their fight when he woke to hear her sobbing. It had been eerie to realize she was asleep. He'd felt guilty, then worse, when touching her had scared the hell out of her.

"It was just a bad dream," she had dismissed after his soothing turned to lovemaking and her soft weight lay pliant against him. Embarrassed, she had risen to make bacon and eggs in the middle of the night.

"You should have told me after the first time," he said now, trying to fit this new information into his vision of her as a lying schemer. His father had tortured Travis in his own way, but it had been by pushing him into a state of passive helplessness. His father had never, ever, deliberately hurt him. Neither of them were the type to be effusive, but he didn't question his father's love or pride in him.

"Why?" she asked between bites. "What would telling you have changed?"

He didn't know. Would he have tried to keep her away from the man? He had known things weren't all roses there. The other time she'd had the dream had been a couple of weeks later, mere days before she'd walked out for good. She'd seen her father and had arrived home late, clearly upset.

He had assumed she didn't want to talk. He hadn't asked why she was so withdrawn.

*You didn't want to know about my life any more than you wanted to share details about yours.*

He hadn't wanted to open up, so he hadn't asked her to. He had preferred to kiss her out of her mood, keeping their sharing to the physical pleasure they offered each other. The times when he had sensed she was looking for more from him, some sort of emotional intimacy, he had withdrawn.

Why? Because his mother had cheated on his father and left. Their divorce had been brutal, the fallout nasty, but he would deny carrying a lifetime of scars. Perhaps he was wary of becoming as besotted with a woman as his dad had been, having seen the damage it could do. Mostly he didn't like to talk about it because it was water under the bridge. And none of what he'd experienced was so bad he had nightmares about it.

He had forgotten all about her nightmares. If he had known that hunger brought them on, he would have woken her to come down for dinner earlier. When he'd seen her asleep in his bed, however, something in him had eased. He'd told himself it was the relief from conflict. He wouldn't have to manage her interactions with his family. Who knew what she would say next? What damage she would cause?

*I'm a bad apple who never should have been born.*

He had made himself catch up on work after his houseguests went to bed, but he hadn't been tired enough to fall asleep once he'd crawled into bed beside her. He had been lying there, fighting memories of the other times they'd shared a bed, when he'd heard her breathing change.

Moments later, she had rolled onto her stomach and sobbed into her pillow as though she couldn't take whatever was being done to her. It was horrible. Of *course* he'd woken her to bring her out of it.

She'd known it was him right away, snuggling into place against him as if no time had lapsed at all, arousing him to the breaking point between one heartbeat and the next, with only the graze of her soft skin against his own. Her hand had moved with delicious familiarity and he'd nearly slipped into the erotic world where only the two of them existed.

He couldn't let her manipulate him like that, though. He had put a stop to her seeking touch and she'd reacted with such a jolt, it had only hit him as she pulled away that she'd still been half-asleep.

The fact her reaction hadn't been a deliberate act of manipulation, but her subconscious still reacting to him, was strangely gratifying. There was a part of him that had wondered if all her responses back then had been manufactured to wring a dollar value out of him, but the sensuality that had so ensnared him had, at least, been real.

"See?" she murmured, brushing her fingers over her plate. "Telling you has just made both of us uncomfortable and it changes nothing." Her cheeks looked hollow, her pleated brow fraught with embarrassment and despair. She rinsed the plate and put it into the dishwasher. "It shouldn't happen again, but I'll sleep down here, just in case."

"Go back to bed."

She gripped her elbows. Her narrow shoulders hunched up. "I don't want to sleep with you."

No? He would dearly love to test that, but only said, "I'll stay down here."

"I don't want to put you out."

He snorted.

The flash of injury in her expression was a bolt of lightning, jagged and searing, lasting only milliseconds but smacking him in the chest, leaving him breathless and seeing nothing while she walked away without even wishing him a good night.

It wasn't.

After tossing and turning, Imogen had slept late, waking to hear Travis in the shower. She went downstairs to find his sister and her family gone.

"Toni took her gifts?" she guessed when he came downstairs.

"Saved me packing them, so I said yes to her taking them."

That was when she learned they were going south to his father's birthday and having Christmas with the bunch of them.

"You can't ask me to participate in that. I can't afford gifts." She hadn't celebrated since her mother and sister had been alive.

"It's very low-key," he said dismissively. "Until the kids came along, we didn't do gifts at all. We still don't exchange between adults. Gwyn bakes cookies and makes a nice dinner."

It would still be awkward and painful, making her feel like an outsider yet again.

She had silently prayed the doctor would caution her against flying, getting her out of it, but an hour later the jerk had peered in her ear and pronounced, "Settling down nicely." He had approved her for travel provided she kept up with her antibiotics.

Since then, Travis had been expediently making decisions on her behalf, seeming to grow more impatient with her by the minute. "Stop asking how much everything costs," he muttered as he herded her along Fifth Avenue. "You need clothes."

"Normal clothes. Not..."

Not designer jeans at two grand a pair and cocktail dresses straight from the cover of *Vogue*. Imogen was currently changing out of a new dress to replace Gwyn's. This one was also a cable-knit, but it clung to her flyweight frame. It was so cute it had her reliving her three-year sentence on the fashion desk.

The cheeky lace-up sides on this forest green sheath add panache to a seasonal standard. Pair with a knee-high dress boot and an open-front trench for a day of shopping, then loosen the skirt laces for cocktails and clubbing.

The snug knit and low neckline flatters the most modest curves. Ramp up the fun factor with a bright red scarf and a bold lip, or drop in some drama with patterned black tights and a boho bracelet.

Now he was badgering her into ever-more-elegant eveningwear. And badgering the boutique's owner while he was at it.

"I don't care if frosted colors are made of titanium and on sale for ninety-nine cents. They're too ashen for her. Bring something vibrant. Jewel tones." He had an artist's eye in a businessman's head. The foundation of his fortune was real estate, built on his father's success in that arena, but Travis's vocation was architecture. He had shot into the stratosphere based on his ability to bring contemporary form and function to classic building design. "Yes, more like that."

An assistant was allowed past his gatekeeper surliness and came into Imogen's spacious changeroom with a sapphire-blue gown draped over her arms.

"Sorry," Imogen murmured on his behalf.

The woman brushed it off with a warm smile. "A day of spoiling is always a treat, isn't it?" She helped Imogen into the dress.

Spoiling? Was that what this was? Imogen was already in French lace underwear the last attendant had forced on her at his command. This didn't feel like indulgence. It felt like an assertion of his wealth and power over her, while putting further obligations upon her.

"Shoes," the young woman decided after zipping her. She hurried away.

"Can't you tell your father I have the plague and leave me here while you go to Charleston?" Imogen asked, poking her head out to where he lounged on a sofa, sipping champagne and scrolling through his phone. "You don't want me to meet him," she reminded him.

"He wants to meet you."

"But I don't know what you're expecting of me. What are the rules?" What was the punishment if she broke them?

"Rule one is to quit fighting me on every little thing." He lifted his gaze. "Let me see."

"It's too long. She's bringing me shoes."

"Get out here."

In all her years of trailing behind her father to galas and award ceremonies, she had never once worn a gown, only cocktail length. Deep down, she was loving this. She felt like a princess with silk whispering against her legs and tickling the tops of her feet. The cut lifted her modest bust and the shade turned her eyes to the color of the Caribbean Sea.

But she wasn't wearing makeup. Her hair was in a ponytail and she was so, so sensitive to his criticism. He had made a face at Gwyn's too-big dress, insisting they find something else immediately, as if he couldn't stand to be seen with her looking less than 110 percent. He had then nodded curtly to accept the green knit, barely looked at the jeans and showed zero interest in her shiny new boots. He wasn't enjoying this. It was something he had to do because she had ruined his life. *Again.*

She devolved into that most primitive of female desires for approval by hoping she looked pretty enough to please him. She picked up the skirt and hesitantly walked out to present herself.

He didn't move except to scan his critical eye up and down her with slow, thorough study. Finally, he took a sip of his champagne and said, "That will do." His gaze went back to his phone.

Her heart sank through the floor. She shifted her weight, standing on that stupid, pulsing organ that wanted and wanted and wanted.

The attendant hurried over with a pair of strappy black heels dangling from her fingers.

"Don't bother." Imogen picked up her skirt and turned to go back into the changeroom, blinking the sting from her eyes.

"Imogen." *Bad girl.* "Try on the shoes."

"Why?" she tossed over her shoulder. "You've made your decision."

The distracted attention he'd been giving her focused in so tightly, she felt the heat of his gaze like a laser that burned patterns into her skin. Like an electric lasso that looped out and held her in place while jolting her with a thousand volts.

"And now I've decided I want to see it with shoes."

The attendant heard the silky danger in his tone and crouched before Imogen. "We'll see if it needs hemming." She eased each of Imogen's feet into the shoes.

Imogen held Travis's gaze the whole time, staring him down even though she had no power here. Even though she was scared spitless of his anger.

*Show no fear.*

The young woman stood back and said, "Oh, yes, that's lovely. Don't you think, sir?"

Imogen waited, holding his gaze, waiting and waiting, while he said *nothing.*

"Would it kill you to be nice for five minutes?" she blurted.

His scathing gaze went down the gown to the French label shoes, coming back with a pithy disdain. He was being more than nice, his askance brow said, spending this kind of money on her.

She tightened her hands into fists. "Just buy me a leash and parade me around naked, then, since all you really want is the ability to yank me to heel."

His expression didn't change except for a bolt of something in his eyes at her temerity. He set aside his glass and stood, dropping his phone onto the cushion as he walked toward her, still holding her gaze. He jerked his head to signal the attendant to make herself scarce.

Imogen's heart pounded, but she held her ground.

"Now you've gone and made it look like we're fighting." He traced his fingertip up the throbbing artery in her throat, ending under her chin to tilt her gaze up to his.

His expression was mild, his eyes glittering with fury.

"And how things look is all you care about, isn't it?" She kept her voice low. "Was I not pretty enough to be your wife? Is that why you were so ashamed of me? Is that why I have to wear all these fancy labels and be seen, not heard?"

His touch shifted to hold her jaw in a gentle but implacable hand. "If I want to stop you talking, I know how to do it."

"Yes, you know all the best ways to hurt me and you can't resist standing on each of those bruises, can you?"

"*Does* it hurt, Imogen?" He lowered his head so his

mouth hovered near her own. "Last night when you reached for me, were you thinking about how good I made you feel? Four years seems a long time to go without sex. I don't believe you have."

The bastard. She ought to shove him away, but when she lifted her hands, it was only to splay them on his sides. She did think about the way he'd made her feel. Had every single day for the four years since she'd last touched him. Of the very few dates she'd been on, none had roused so much as a desire to kiss another man.

"You've been throwing it around like hard candy at a parade, I suppose?"

"Want some?" He slanted his head to take one microscopic nibble of her bottom lip.

The tiny contact strummed through her in a tremor of acute need.

This did hurt, but she was losing track of whether this was the pain of his derision or the pain of not having what she craved more than anything.

Her hands shifted, splaying wider to feel more of him while sliding to his waist and pressing. Encouraging him to come closer. Trying to pull herself into him.

"I do," she said in a thready voice, knowing it was a mistake to offer herself. She half expected him to shove her away, triumphant.

Instead, an atavistic light filled his gaze. His hand shifted to catch behind her neck and he crushed her mouth with his own, hot and possessive.

His other arm went around her and her chest collided with his. Time folded. The past crunched into the present and exploded into golden light and shattered defenses. Panic should have been her reaction, but all she felt was relief. Oh, he was rain after a long drought. Her whole being filled up with rejuvenation, swelling and reaching and opening for him. This man was the only one who did this to her, mind spinning away so all that mattered was that she wear his spicy scent on every inch of her skin. That he gather her into his powerful physique and ravage her with a hunger only exceeded by her own.

She twined her arms around his neck and pulled him down, encouraging the pressure of his mouth to the point of pain, trying to erase the ache of longing that had held her in its grip these four long years.

He met her anguished yearning with a ravenous type of control, body so hot around hers, she stood in a conflagration while he blatantly dove his tongue into her mouth. She was his. His action seemed to drive it home to her.

She couldn't deny it. She kissed him back without inhibition, greeting his tongue with her own, rubbing against him in open invitation. *Take me. All of me.*

It was exactly the way she had given herself over to him every time in the past. Even as she was cringing inside at her wantonness while celebrating the joy of being back in his arms, he was dragging his hands to her shoulders and pressing her away.

Her knees were too soft. She had to cling to his wrists to stay on her feet. It was mortifying.

His expression was avid and flushed. Aroused? Maybe. But sharp and accusatory, too. Angry but smug. He'd been teaching her a lesson.

Well, all she'd learned was that she couldn't trust either of them.

"I actually hate you right now," she told him in whatever was left of her voice. Then she carefully turned and closed herself into the changeroom so he wouldn't see that her lashes were growing as damp as the rest of her.

# CHAPTER FIVE

"WE'RE DONE FOR TODAY," Travis said over his shoulder to the women standing across the room and pretending not to goggle at his spectacle with Imogen. "Package everything up."

He took out his credit card, drained his champagne, and went back to reading work emails so he wouldn't follow Imogen into the changeroom and finish what they'd started.

*I actually hate you right now.*

Given that he was lurking in the back of the boutique, waiting for a raging erection to subside, he was feeling quite a bit of animosity toward her, too.

He'd barely slept, trying to assimilate all that she'd told him last night with the way he'd viewed her all these years. Would things have been different if she'd told him? He was annoyed that he didn't know and hadn't been given a chance to find out.

Then she'd balked at going to Charleston and was pushing back on him with every purchase he was making, further shortening his temper.

Meanwhile, he'd been going out of his mind, watching her try on tight jeans that cupped her pert behind. He'd tried not to notice her bare knee between the hem of her skirt and the top of her boot when she sat beside him in the car or the way the neckline of her new dress framed the upper swells of her breasts. It reminded him too much of the way her soft body had felt slithering close to his oh-so-briefly last night.

When she had walked out in a gown that turned her skin to rich cream, one that made her hair catch lights and shadows and transformed her eyes into mysterious pools while it lovingly showcased the delicacy of her figure, he'd been almost beside himself with latent arousal.

And she wanted him to be *nice* to her? Nothing about this was *nice*. It was base and frustrating and colored with dark emotions he couldn't seem to identify.

"I'm ready." She appeared in the green dress, her waist so impossibly narrow, the gold belt sat like a small Hula-Hoop atop her hips. He kept forgetting how sick she'd been, but her face was pale enough to remind him.

He looked for the fire of defiance beneath her mask of obedience, the one that kept lighting his own temper, keeping him fighting. He waited for a sneer of sarcasm, but all he saw was tension and a hint of redness lingering on her lips from their rapacious kiss. She didn't meet his eyes, only offered a wan smile to the shop owner. "Thank you for all your help. I'll wait in the car."

Travis walked her out, leaving his driver to deal with the packages.

"What game are we playing now?" he asked as she turned her face away from him the moment he slid in beside her and closed the door. "Silent treatment?"

"Of course not. What would you like to talk about?"

She folded her hands in her lap and brought her face to the front, but this woman had never been so polite.

"You're angry that I kissed you," he surmised.

"Of course not," she said in that same ultrareasonable tone that was ultraprovoking in a passive-aggressive way. "You've demonstrated that you are allowed to do whatever you please with me."

Behind them, the driver closed the trunk. It shook the car, but the real impact was that precise little shot she'd taken with her loaded words.

When the driver opened his door, Travis barked, "Give us a minute."

"Of course, sir." He closed the door and moved to the curb in front of the car, shooing away the handful of photographers who'd been tracking them today.

"You didn't enjoy that kiss? It was something I *took*? Is that what you're saying?" The clench in his belly tightened.

"Whether I enjoyed it doesn't matter, does it? That was the point you were making. Whatever you do to me is a reaction—punishment—for what I did and continue to do to you." Her voice shook and her knuckles were white until she very deliberately relaxed her hands, drawing a breath that she let out in a slow measured exhalation. Like she was enduring something intensely painful.

"It wasn't a punishment, Imogen." Unless—*I actually hate you right now*. "*Did* you enjoy it?" His heart lurched, wondering if he had actually gone insane because he'd been sure they were both reacting with exactly as much passion as the other.

"Yes." Her voice belied that clipped answer. "You could have had me right there in the middle of the floor in a shop. Is that what you need to hear? Does that make you happy? How much is enough, Travis? How completely do you have to humiliate me before I'm sorry enough for ever having entered your life?"

She finally looked at him, but her eyes shone with angry tears. Shame raked at his conscience with sharp claws.

"I wasn't trying to humiliate you."

"Right," she said scathingly, hand turning into a fist again. "Just tell me the rules and I'll stop breaking them. The penance isn't worth it."

"It wasn't…" Agitation had him turning in his seat toward her.

She tensed. Braced herself. Winded him with the very idea that—

"I'm not going to hit you!"

"I didn't think you were," she claimed, but she held herself in wary stiffness, her sharp gaze on his.

He ran his hand down his face, trying to get a grip while his brain went ballistic.

He still wasn't sure what to make of the things she had said about her father last night. She hadn't said anything about violence, and he didn't believe she would have tried so hard to win over a man who had raised his fists against her. It had sounded more like her father was withdrawn and bitter, perhaps from grief, capable of lashing out, but Imogen was a dramatic person. He had wondered if she had exaggerated, trying to earn sympathy and forgiveness. She had flat out warned him against believing her.

But this reaction of hers was pure instinct and dread inducing in the extreme. He didn't even want to ask, let alone hear the answer, but he made himself do it.

"Did he hit you? Your father?" He would dig him up and kill him again.

"No."

"Imogen."

"Stop saying my name like that."

*"It's your name."*

"And you say it like I'm stupid and wrong and you can't stand me. You don't have to use your fists to hurt people, Travis." Her elbows were tight to her ribs, her body so tense she looked like she would snap.

*The runt is the one who is supposed to drown.*

He didn't want to believe her father had been that cruel because he would have to face that he had let her go back to Wallace. Had driven her there. His nostrils stung and a bonfire of culpability burned under his heart.

"Just tell me the rules and I'll follow them," she said again, voice strained. "Don't contradict you in public. Wear what you buy me. What else?"

"Imo—"

She flinched.

He closed his eyes. Gentled his tone, even though she was so infuriating he could barely control himself. "This isn't a test. It's not tennis. I wasn't trying to score a point with that kiss." Not entirely a lie. He had just wanted to *know* whether her reaction in the past had been real or manufactured.

"You're going to find fault in me no matter what I do. At least give me a fighting chance because I can't live with being smacked down all the time. You want me to act like we're in love when we're in public? Is that what I'm supposed to do?"

He scratched his brow. Sighed.

She flinched and looked away.

Really? She was so sensitive that a noise of frustration was a lash of a whip?

"Imogen." He managed to say it softly. His hand twitched to reach out, but he was afraid to touch her now, uncertain how she would take it, how she would feel it, wound as tightly as she was. He had never in all this time imagined he had the power to hurt her. Not that deeply.

"Do you expect me to have sex with you?" Her unsteady voice held a throb that sent a spear of aching tension through him.

"I don't expect it, no." Want? Yes. How the hell had things disintegrated into this?

"Because I don't know how to make it 'interesting'?" Her face was turned away, but her hand came up to swipe her cheek. "I was busy trying to help Dad. Taking care of him was a full-time job around my real one. That's why I didn't sleep with anyone else. I mean, I went out a few times, but just the odd dinner. So, yes, it has been a long time and that's why I reacted today, okay?"

She said it with enough vehemence he knew she was just trying to save face with him, but it still landed and stung. He had damned near devoured her and he hadn't been going without.

"I'm not built for casual sex. I don't know why. It's always bothered me."

Every single word this woman said baffled the hell out of him. "Why would you aspire to be good at casual sex?"

"Because it would be nice to connect with someone without getting hurt."

"If you're saying I was too rough, I'm—"

"Shut *up*, Travis. You don't expect to have sex with me. Fine. Do you expect me to pay you back for these clothes? That's why I kept asking how much—"

"No," he cut in, pinching the bridge of his nose. "You need clothes. Stop asking what I expect. I expect you to let me help you back onto your feet and not get yourself into another situation like this again. I expect you to take care of yourself and eat when you're hungry and get enough sleep and take your medication. If I sound overbearing and frustrated it's because I cannot believe you let things get to this level and that you're fighting me on fixing them."

Her mouth was pouted, her brow cringing at his harsh tone while her jaw worked, searching for a defense. "I don't want you to resent me more than you do."

"Well, you're going to love my next demand, because I expect you to tell me how much you owe so I can take care of it."

"No." Her knuckles stood out sharp and white on her tight fists.

"Your debt collectors are calling my office. I have to address it."

"You're not responsible for what I owe! Definitely not for what my father racked up."

"They don't care who pays, as long as they get their money." Keeping his father's business going when it had teetered on the brink had taught him exactly how financial vultures worked, compounding late fees faster than you could write a check. "We can do this the easy way or the hard way, Imogen. The easy way is for you to give me a list and we zero it off, quick and neat. The interest is the killer, so the longer you put it off, the worse it gets."

She scowled and hung her head. "I don't—" she began.

"It's like the debt clock," he cut in dryly. "While you waffle, it keeps rolling higher."

"Okay, fine! I'll need to go online when we get back to your apartment, but can we go somewhere first? I want to give you something. At least I can get that much off my conscience."

"What?"

"Your rings."

By the time they had driven to the converted brownstone in Brooklyn, where a handful of windows were framed with strings of colored lights, he had stopped speaking to her at all.

"I didn't feel desperate enough to sell them" had been the words that had flipped his switch into incensed silence. She had heard what he was thinking, though. Had known he was picturing that horrible little room in the sauerkraut-smelling building. If that wasn't desperation, what was?

Imogen bit her lip as they climbed from the car in front of Joli's building. If Joli wasn't home, Travis was really going to lose his bananas, but he'd been so busy taking her to task for "starving on the street," she hadn't wanted to get into the fact that, without her old cell phone and its helpful contact list, she didn't have Joli's number.

She buzzed the apartment with Joli's name on the plate and thankfully Joli answered.

"It's Imogen."

"I wondered if you would turn up. Come in."

"Who is she?" Travis asked as they climbed the stairs of the modest but well-kept building. This one smelled like nutmeg and cinnamon, thanks to neighbors preparing for the holidays.

"One of Dad's editors. She was a freelance journalist for years and went back to it after our flagship folded. She sent condolences when Dad died, but we haven't been in touch much since she went out on her own again."

As they arrived on the third floor, a door opened. Joli was heavyset and wore her gray hair in a no-nonsense, flat, boyish cut combed straight down on her forehead. Glasses that needed cleaning and a cigarette hanging out of her mouth were pretty much her signature look.

"How are you, kid?" She nodded at Imogen. Not the affectionate type, far too analytical and objective as a lifelong newsperson, but a trusted ally for years.

"The architect," Joli said when Imogen introduced Travis. "When I saw your names in the headlines this morning, I dug up your article on him and reread it."

"What? Why?" Maybe the bigger question was *how?*

Joli's studio apartment bordered on something from those shows about hoarders. Filing cabinets were covered in stacks of thick folders and surrounded by bulging cardboard boxes. Her kitchen table was a layered workspace of cuttings and notepads. Papers with brown mug rings sat on the coffee table while her desk in the corner was a computer poking above a mountain of spiral notebooks, colored index cards and full ashtrays. The whole place reeked of stale cigarette smoke.

"Bit flowery," Joli said with a wink, retrieving a

few pages from next to her computer. "But solid. He should have printed it." She offered them to Imogen.

"Oh, no—"

"Thank you." Travis took the papers and folded them in half.

"Travis," Imogen protested, trying to take the pages.

He ignored her, folded them again and tucked them inside his suit jacket.

She tightened her mouth and turned back to Joli. "I came for my rings. Do you mind?"

"In the fire safe." Joli crossed to the safe beneath her desk. She bent to dial it open. "Who are you working for these days?"

"I'm not writing. I had to sell my computer."

Travis sent her a frown.

Imogen shrugged. "It would have been stolen otherwise. At least the cash fit in my bra."

His next question should have been "What bra?" but the cash was long gone, too.

He asked instead, "Is that why the rings are here? You were afraid they'd be stolen?"

"I used to leave them with Joli when I went into the office, so Dad wouldn't see them. He would have told me to sell them."

Joli picked through old tapes and USBs, then came across a sealed envelope that had Property of Imogen Gantry written in bold print across it.

Imogen tore the envelope open and waited for Travis to offer his hand, which he did very slowly, radiating skepticism. She poured the rings into his palm, where the two bands sat like a platinum figure eight. An infinity sign weighted on one side with baguette diamonds, a pillow-cut stone with matched baguettes on the other.

She loved those rings. *Loved* them.

Which was why she hadn't been able to bring herself to sell them, no matter how dire her circumstances. It was heartbreaking enough to return them to the man who'd given them to her. She had to do it without touching them, without even looking at them for very long, or she might cry.

It wasn't even because they were so beautiful. They were stunning, but it was what they had meant when he gave them to her. What she had believed they meant. As fairy tales went, they had symbolized a happily-ever-after commitment that was pure and bright and magical. Sometimes she'd wondered if her biggest mistake had been in taking them off every day, hiding them from everyone and only wearing them in the privacy of Travis's apartment. Maybe if she had worn them around the clock, the spell would have stuck.

And maybe she had a rich imagination.

She handed the torn envelope to Joli. "I'd love some freelance work if you have any leads. Ad copy, anything."

"Email me," Joli said in her gravelly voice.

"Thanks."

Travis waited until they were in the car to say, "You said you didn't have any friends to lean on."

"Did it look like she has disposable income or a sofa I could use?" She made a face. "She's very independent and wouldn't dream of asking anyone for anything, except maybe what I just asked for—tips and leads. I knew if I went to her for money, she'd tell me to sell the rings and I didn't want to."

He had tucked them into his pocket and sat with his elbow on the armrest, finger resting across his lips. "Explain that to me again." The exaggerated patience in his tone grated; it was so supercilious.

She shrugged. "As long as I had them, I felt like I had *something*. I wasn't at zero. Also, selling them wouldn't have made a dent in the debt, so what was the point in giving them up and still being broke?"

He was searching her expression, picking apart her words. She could feel it and held her breath, realizing she had been hanging on to this link to him, needing it.

She decided to change the subject, even though it meant asking for another favor.

"It would be helpful..." she began, twisting her hands in her lap. "I mean, if you're serious about helping me get on my feet, it would be helpful if I could borrow a computer. I've kept a toe in with freelancing. It was just hard to hustle work when I had to get to the library around my other jobs. Half the time they kick you off after an hour and I wasn't picking up my emails fast enough. I'd get back to people only to hear they'd already offered it to someone else."

A beat of surprise, then he nodded. "I'll buy you a laptop."

"Just a loan. Please."

He only reached into his jacket. She thought he was getting his phone, but he pulled out the pages Joli had given him.

"Don't read that!"

He hesitated. "Why not?"

"Because I don't want to know how you react."

"How do you expect me to react? She said it was good, didn't she?"

She jerked a protective shoulder. "I wrote it when things were very different between us. I don't—don't want to see your reaction. Put it away."

"When we first met, I thought you were unlike anyone I'd ever met before." He folded the pages and tucked them back into his pocket. "I still don't understand you."

"I'm defensive. I wouldn't think I'd need to spell that out. I'm afraid you'll think that article is too full of awe. You'll see again what a green, starstruck little fool I was and laugh at me for it. If that's how you get off, go ahead." She waved with annoyance at his lapel. "Get it over with, then."

He lifted his brows. "Can I suggest something to you? Your father is dead. You don't have to denigrate yourself in his absence."

Nice advice, but it was going to be humiliating no matter what. He would realize how much he had meant to her and might even guess how gutted she was now. That would make today's kiss and his rejection that much more intolerable. Maybe he deserved to know how full of regret she was, but it was too mortifying to still be half in love with a man who had never cared for her at all.

"Is that why your father refused to publish it? Did he think it was biased?"

"I doubt he even read it." The cityscape grew as they crossed the bridge.

She felt his stare and turned her head to see something smoldering in his dark expression, something that made her abdomen tense.

"You should have told me how bad it was, Imogen."

"It doesn't matter," she muttered, looking away, hurt

for some reason. Maybe because his reaction was too little, too late. Maybe because she was angry with herself for not confiding in him. "There's no changing it. I'm over it."

He raised his brows in disbelief.

"That's why I was starting over the way I was," she defended. "Yes, it was the hard way, but I didn't want anything from my past to come with me. Nothing connected to him. That's why I carried my marriage certificate. At least I could pretend I had your name instead of his."

Hours later, Travis was spending way too much time lifting his gaze from his screen to the view out the door of his office. Not to look at the tree, either.

They'd come home to a lounge put back in order, toys stowed in the closet again, wet wipes back under the sink in the powder room.

Travis had bought a new laptop on the way home, which Imogen had taken to the sofa after changing into tights and a long sweater. She kept shifting, bending and straightening her legs so the hem of her sweater fell to reveal the slenderness of her thighs. She absently pushed it back toward her knee and rubbed one socked foot over the other. They were fuzzy white socks that made him want to squeeze her arches and toes like one of Toni's plush stuffies. She played with her hair, tickling the fanned end against her thoughtfully pursed lips. She arched and plumped the pillow behind her back, pushing her breasts against the knit of her blue sweater, then relaxed with a soft sigh that vibrated through him all the way over here.

Fantasies of walking out there, taking that laptop

from her startled hands, settling over her and making love to her on the sofa consumed him.

Their kiss earlier was still clouding his brain and now he had a pair of rings and her article to confound him along with the rest of what she'd revealed. It all spun him back to the heated moments in the back of his car the night before they married. They'd been parked outside her building, his driver having a cigarette somewhere. He'd had his hand up her skirt and she'd been trembling from the most exquisite orgasm he'd ever witnessed.

He would have done anything, *anything* in that moment. It was all he could do to restrain himself from claiming her completely right there in the street. Instead he commanded grittily, "Invite me up."

Their clothes had been askew, her body still quivering and damp, her lips parted as she tried to catch her breath. When her eyes blinked open in the light through the fogged windows, they'd been hazed with lust.

Something like agony had pleated her brow and she had bitten her bottom lip before she swallowed and lowered her lashes in a kind of defeat. "If that's what you want."

They had been nose to nose, the air charged with intimacy. Every nuance and breath had imprinted on him—not that he had let himself revisit that memory in the time that had since passed. It was far more comfortable to resent her as a world-class manipulator.

If he had been manipulated, however, it had been his own hormones and conscience.

"Isn't that what you want?" he had asked.

She'd been honey and heat, pliant with surrender

against him, lips clinging to his as he'd succumbed to the need to taste her mouth once more, keeping the fire burning hot between them. Caressing her so she'd gasped and arched in offering.

"It is." Her voice had throbbed with longing. "But I was saving it for my husband. For a man who—" She had buried the rest into his neck, her damp mouth making his scalp tighten.

A man who what? Loved her? His hand on her mound had firmed with possessiveness as he felt pulled apart. In those moments, he had only half believed she was a virgin. Her shocked gasp under his initial bold touch, however, and the way she had shattered with shy joy, inclined him to think she'd never let anyone touch her this intimately before.

As he'd continued fondling and necking with her, he hadn't seen her virginity as the prize so much as feeling irrationally jealous at the idea of her being with other men. He had wanted to make her his in a way that went beyond the physical.

As she'd rested her head on his arm and gazed up at him with surrender, he'd read the melancholy in her trembling smile.

He could have pressed her to let him have her that night. He could have taken her virginity without the rings, but she would have regretted it. On some level, she would have felt cheapened by giving in without a commitment between them.

*Travis Sanders's lay of the day.*

His stomach tightened as he recalled how that hadn't been enough for him, either. Not in those moments. So, he had said the words. *Marry me. Tomorrow.* He'd spent the night drawing up the prenuptial agreement, thinking he was being sensible in the midst of pure recklessness.

"That's it." Her voice snapped him back to his office while a ping at his elbow notified him of yet another email arriving.

She was talking about the folders and links and contacts she'd been sending him over the last hour. Now she stood in the doorway and glanced around the office he rarely used. His real office was only blocks away and he traveled to site so often that when he was in his actual home, he preferred to unplug and unwind.

Imogen's gaze narrowed on the folded papers he'd left on the corner of his desk. She hugged herself defensively. "Did you read it?"

"No," he lied, not ready to confront his feelings on how she'd portrayed him and revealed herself. Straightening, he pulled himself back to the immediate matter at hand. "I've been messaging with my accountant. He said at first blush there are several items that should be settled as part of your father's estate and not carried over to you."

She made a face of mild disgust. "I knew I should have hired an accountant, but won't their fees wash out whatever he saves me?"

"We'll see. He's preparing a release for you to sign, to let his office take over the probate of your father's will. He said the service provided by the home where your father passed is fine for seniors with modest assets, but they're not the right approach for something this complex."

"All right." She curled her socked toes. "Do you want me to see if there are steaks or something in the freezer for dinner?"

That wasn't the appetite gnawing so consistently at him.

*It would be nice to connect with someone without getting hurt.*

Wouldn't it?

"We'll go out." His voice sounded more gravelly and curt than he intended, making her stiffen and scowl warily.

"Why?"

She was entitled to her shock, and he had ulterior motives, but it bothered him that she was so suspicious. That he couldn't ask her to dinner without it being a thing that stirred up their past. This constant unraveling of threads he'd long thought tied off was exhausting. Especially since each thread was a viper that ended with a bite and a sting of poison. He sincerely wished they could move forward into something that wasn't so fraught.

"We're promoting a vision of reconciliation," he reminded her. "At least, the press release implies we're having a fresh try."

Her brows went up in a silent and disparaging, "Good luck with that."

He pushed aside his phone and rested his forearms on the desk.

"How things look *is* important to me. Partly it's who I am. Look around. I run a tidy ship. One of the reasons we went out first thing this morning was to give the housekeeper a chance to wipe down all the furniture. The kids make a mess and it's all I can do to wait until they're gone to clean up after them."

"You're a neat freak?" She looked at him in sudden

interest, mouth curving into a teasing smile. "Here I thought you were perfect."

"Worse. I'm a perfection*ist*."

Her smile didn't stick. Her humor dimmed and her lashes swept to hide her eyes. Because she wasn't perfect? Neither was he, much to his chagrin.

"It's my biggest flaw, but I come by it honestly. My mother spent my entire childhood wiping my face and hands, smoothing my hair and straightening my tie."

Imogen bit back a smile. "I may require photo evidence of that. Please tell me it was a bow tie."

"I was every bit as fastidious as she was. When I started high school, my father said he would give me a dollar per mark, provided I kept my grades above seventy percent. Who wants a pile of bills adding up to ninety-eight when you can have a crisp Ben Franklin?"

"There are easier ways to a skinny wallet, you know. Kind of an expert over here." She gave a little wave. "Ask me anything."

And here was the woman who had led him off his straight and narrow path into a wilderness of unpredictability. He forced himself to stay focused on what he wanted to convey.

"I was the school's top track athlete, I headed the debate team, played saxophone and organized a repair of a seniors' center after a storm damaged it."

"And dated the head cheerleader?" It was an accurate guess, but he wasn't stupid enough to confirm it.

"I also worked weekends at my father's office and assisted with conveyancing contracts. You can't miss dotting an *i* on those. I was voted best all-around student two years in a row. My life was as flawless as I could make it, my future paved in gold."

He ran his tongue over his teeth, getting to the difficult bit.

"Then my mother had a blazing affair. She shattered my father's heart and handed me a cloud of filthy rumors to wear as I finished out my high school years. Dad nearly lost his business and I had to drop my extracurricular activities to look after him."

Her smile faded and her gaze softened with concern. "Sick?"

"Alcohol."

"I'm so sorry."

He didn't want her pity. This was an explanation, not a therapy session.

"My marks suffered, which was untenable, and I got kicked out of school twice for fighting. I *hate* gossip and bad press, Imogen. I hate even more when I lower myself into reacting to it. I prefer to keep a tight control over myself and everything around me so it never comes to that."

Her mouth twitched. "I've noticed that. You play your cards close to your chest so you're always one square ahead of everyone else."

He narrowed his eyes at her. "You mixed that metaphor on purpose, didn't you? Knowing it would bother me. This is why you make me crazy."

"There could be a board game that uses cards and spaces. I don't know." She pretended innocence with a lift of her gaze to the ceiling.

That was the part that got to him. The mischief. The invitation to laugh at himself. He shouldn't be drawn to such capriciousness and maybe that's why he'd held back from truly committing to their marriage. He couldn't spend a lifetime with this much uncertainty. With a woman who wasn't 1,000 percent steady. In a moment of madness, he had wanted to lock her down, contain her, but he had quickly realized such a thing was impossible.

"I didn't expect our marriage to last," he admitted. "You're right about that."

Her lighthearted half smile died. She had one hand on the doorjamb and quarter-turned into it, looking as if she would rather walk away than hear this. Her profile paled, despite the warmth of the gas fireplace having left color in her cheeks a moment ago. She drew her bottom lip between her teeth.

"After witnessing the way my parents' marriage imploded, I knew I didn't want anything to leave a stain on me when ours fell apart." Maybe he'd even pulled what few supports they had had, encouraging it to collapse so he wouldn't have to wait for the inevitable. "We're very different, Imogen."

"I'm not perfect."

"You're creative. That's not a bad thing."

"You're creative," she pointed out.

"In a disciplined way."

"The right way."

Why her saying that wrung out his internal organs, he wasn't sure.

"Then why—?" Her voice cracked and she looked upward again.

The artist in him admired the beautiful line from her profile, down her throat and along her feminine torso to the curve of her waist. Artwork. She was absolute beauty without even trying. He took a mental picture, wanting to replicate that line somehow, somewhere. His muse.

Something deep within him kept wanting to preserve these moments of striking beauty she produced, the sound of her laugh, the scent in a room she had recently occupied. He wanted to press each memory into a book. Secure them in a safe.

But he couldn't. He had known that the first time and knew it even more indelibly now. A woman like her wasn't meant to be confined. It was beyond wrong.

He heard the vestiges of pain in her voice as she tried again and this time succeeded with voicing her question, if faintly.

"Why do you want to parade this messy *ex*-wife of yours in public? Shouldn't I be kept behind closed doors?"

Locked in her room, missing dinner.

The twisting, wringing sensation in him wrenched to an excruciating tightness. His chest grew compressed. "Gwyn's debacle arrived as I was expanding and taking on debt for a massive project in South America."

"The cathedral."

"For the Catholic church, yes. You can imagine how thrilled they were that my sister was being publicly shamed for nude photos and a raging affair with a banker. Please don't ever tell her how bad it was. She was going through far worse, but it demonstrated to me exactly how important my image is to my clients. I'm closing on something in Hawaii as soon as the holidays are over. I can't risk their confidence flagging because they fear I'm having personal problems."

"So, put on my Sunday best, mind my manners and clean up the mess I've made."

"I own some of this mess, Imogen. I know that."

"Because you never should have married me." She

was looking at her hand now, where she played her thumb against the plate of the catch. In a sudden move, she pulled her hand away and pressed her thumb to her mouth.

"Did you just cut yourself?" How? She really was a disaster waiting to happen.

"No," she lied around her thumb, scowling at him. "What time do I need to be ready?"

"Let me see." He rose.

"I'm a big girl. I can solve my own problems." She held her ground, tucking her thumb inside her fist and dropping her hand, not hearing the ridiculousness of her statement when his email was ringing like a stock trading bell with notes and questions from his accountant about her catastrophe of a financial situation.

Maybe she did hear it, though. She lowered her gaze and her shoulders heaved in a defeated sigh.

He gave her this one and stayed where he was.

"We have reservations for seven. Check the powder room for bandages."

She walked away and down the hall.

*You look lovely.*

Imogen was trying not to smooth her dress down her hips or fiddle with the neckline as they entered the restaurant. Her mind kept playing a loop of his quiet compliment as they'd left the penthouse. Was he pandering to her fragile self-worth after her hissy fit at the boutique? Making a comment on the fact she didn't look like death warmed over now that she was on the mend? Or had he meant it?

Maybe he was just being polite. Maybe she did look nice. She had always scrubbed up pretty well. Along with all the clothes, some makeup had been delivered. With her hair washed and styled, she looked as good as she could. This dress didn't hurt one bit, either. It was a figure-hugging crepe in panels of purple and ivory with a saucy zipper all the way down the front. Her shoes were a stunning confection of crystals forming a floral embellishment on an otherwise nude mesh with a sparkly heel. Chic and classy, but cheeky.

She desperately wanted to click them together to see if she could fix her life in a blink. On the other hand, this Technicolor world of his, where her mother's change purse had been replaced with a half dozen handbags with designer labels, was a nice place to visit. Even on her best day, she had never carried as much cash in her bank balance as the value of this quilted satin clutch, with its seed pearls in paisley patterns and enameled clasp.

Had he spoken with a hint of emotion in his tone when he'd delivered that succinct compliment? Or had it just sounded that way because she'd been so terribly desperate that he *not* find fault? Had he been forcing the words out? Was it a pity compliment?

Was she that far gone she was okay with that?

"The other half of your party is here. Let me show you to your table," the maître d' said, weaving them through the crush at the front of the restaurant to what seemed an exclusive section at the back, where tables overlooked Central Park. She had glanced longingly at the merrily lit-up carriages trotting down the paths there as they'd entered.

Watching them would be almost as good, but she balked and caught at Travis's arm. "Other half?"

"I invited a friend and his wife, someone willing to help with our PR problem."

*Our?* He wasn't doing *her* reputation any harm. She was the one dragging *him* into the dirt.

As Imogen recognized the couple waiting for them, and they stood for introductions, she must have dug in her heels because Travis's hand in her lower back firmed, pressing her forward exactly as her mother used to when she had wanted Imogen to greet her father after a business trip with a hug and a kiss.

"Nic. Rowan." Travis greeted his guests, then introduced her simply as, "Imogen."

"Gantry," she supplied. Nic Marcussen owned one of the largest news organizations *in the world*. His wife had been a child performer and was the daughter of a well-known starlet from British stage and films. "My father was Wallace Gantry. Travis may have neglected to mention that."

"He didn't have to," Nic said. "I know who you are. I don't have any hard feelings. My sympathies for your loss."

"I suppose professional rivalry is only an issue for the person in second place," she murmured dryly, making him release a surprised chuckle, then give her a look of reassessment.

Maybe he was amused because she had exaggerated her father's position. He'd been running dead last in their particular race, writing more than one inflammatory piece about rivals like Marcussen Media ruining publishing by encouraging the online platform. Meanwhile Nic had evolved with the times and had risen to the top. He could have gloated about that, but he allowed the conversation to move to other topics.

Imogen remained on guard, though, barely touching her wine and filtering every word that left her tongue. It wasn't the other couple that made her so tense. They were witty and relaxed and clearly in love, talking up their children and what sounded like such a perfect life that Imogen's heart contracted with envy.

While she felt like she was being tested with Travis looking at her each time she spoke, making her feel picked apart. She had lived her entire life like this, conscious of how she reflected on her father. Maybe she would have felt this same sense of being on display when she and Travis were married if they'd ever left his apartment, but one of the things that had drawn her to him most inexorably had been a sense that, when she was alone with him, she could be herself, accepted for exactly who she was.

No longer. As forthright as she'd been in the last two days, as much as she had owned up to her mistakes and tried to make amends, she continued to feel as though she fell short. It was agonizing, not that she let on, chuckling on cue and pretending the brush of Travis's thigh against her knee didn't turn her insides to butter.

They were starting dessert when Nic said, "Strong piece on the builder." He was speaking to her, but nodded to indicate he was referring to Travis.

"What?" The heat of a thousand suns swiveled onto her, drying her throat into an arid wasteland. She shot an accusatory look at the man beside her.

"You didn't tell her you sent it to me?" Nic asked.

Travis's flat smile at Nic said, "Thanks a lot."

"You said—" *Behave, Imogen.* She willed the pressure behind her eyes to stay there and looked to her crème brûlée. "He didn't," she replied with a forced smile. "Thank you."

She quickly changed the subject, asking after their home in Greece, and managed to get through the rest of the meal without snapping, but the short trip back to Travis's penthouse was a silence thick with the fulminating anger she was suppressing. She was trembling by the time they were in the elevator.

"I sent it across to him because I thought it was very—"

"I don't care what you thought," she cut in. "You *lied*."

"About reading it? Or about our reason for going to dinner?"

"Both."

"Look, I sent the press release on our reconciliation directly to him, as an exclusive. In return, he made a point of being seen with me, which telegraphs that any smear campaigns against me will have consequences."

The doors opened and she charged straight up the stairs to the guest room she had commandeered.

He followed and stuck out a foot to stop the bedroom door she tried to slam in his face.

She glared at him as she threw down her overpriced, mostly empty clutch—biggest lipstick holder in the history of accessories—and kicked off her insanely expensive shoes without care for their quality.

"Since he and I were on the topic of *you*," Travis continued relentlessly, "I sent across your article, requesting he forward it to one of his editors if he saw a place where you might fit. You seemed interested in freelance work."

"That's not how it works, Travis. Writers are a dime

a dozen and you have to earn your stripes. Do *your* friends send sketches from their wives for you to consider for your next big project, so they don't have to go through the pesky process of apprenticing at the drafting table? No. You expect them to climb through the ranks like everyone else."

"You've paid your dues. Why are you angry? He *liked* it."

"Great! Now what happens if he throws some work my way? Who do I owe for *that*?" She gave a useless pound of her fists into the air at her hips, making her elbows hurt. "You? *Again?*"

"You owe yourself because it was a good piece." He looked confused, like he genuinely didn't understand why he had to explain this to her. "It was thorough, insightful and entertaining."

"I don't care what you thought," she insisted, talking over him.

"Why the hell not?"

"Because you didn't care *then* how I felt about you. I don't need to hear *now* that you find those feelings quaint and pathetic."

He rocked back on his heels, expression shuttering. "That's not what I thought *at all*. For God's sake, Imogen, I thought it sounded as if—"

"It doesn't matter what you think it sounds like! I am being brutally honest with you at every turn," she cried shakily, throwing out her arms in agitation. "I have no ego left. No defenses, no self-worth. I've lost everything and I depend solely on you." She pointed at him in emphasis. "And you lied to me. I asked you if you'd read it and you *lied*."

He pushed his hands into his pockets and looked

away. The ceiling light was on, along with the one in the hallway. There was nowhere for either of them to hide.

"Do I not even deserve honesty from you?" Her whole body throbbed with agony at how little respect that showed.

A muscle pulsed in his jaw before he finally admitted quietly, through his clenched teeth, "I felt naked when I read it."

"*You* did," she choked, dipping her head to rub her brow. "Those were my gauche feelings on display, not *yours*."

"You—" He looked away. "Reading it made me remember the excitement and enthusiasm you showed when we met. I remember how encouraging you were. It was infectious and, yes, flattering." His fists were round bulges in his pockets. "You also captured how *I* was feeling. My passion and ambition for the future. All the aspirations I had for the company. It was uncomfortable to look back on that, mostly because I've lost some of that glossy outlook. I've become cynical and business focused. Reading it was like reading a letter from myself, reminding me why I pushed to expand, what I had hoped to accomplish. It was disturbing to see how far I've strayed from where I intended to be right now."

She searched his expression, which was closed off and resistant to telling her any of this. She wanted to ask where he thought he should be, but only said, "You lied because you didn't want to tell me that?"

"I don't process things as quickly as you do. I have to deconstruct before I can reconstruct. But if you want honesty, Imogen, my first thought was that I needed to thank you for documenting that time in my life. Reading that article renewed my sense of inspiration."

She blinked, feeling for the first time since she'd seen him again that maybe she did have something to offer him.

"At the same time, it was a gentle rebuke." He frowned. "Suddenly, I'm realizing why I haven't been entirely happy with my work lately. I forgot the passion that drove me to architecture in the first place. So, yes, I lied to you while I filtered through all of that."

For some reason, her stomach was full of butterflies, all flitting in different directions, tickling her heart and making her breaths feel unsteady. She didn't know how to process this, either. She was touched. Truly moved by having had some effect on him at all.

She tried to gloss over it by being flippant. "Does that mean I should say 'I'm sorry' or 'you're welcome'?"

"You can say 'you're welcome,'" he said with a sincerity that turned the floor beneath her to sand. "But maybe 'thank you,' as well, since I loathe revealing my missteps, but I sent the article to Nic anyway. I knew it was a stellar example of your ability. I couldn't refuse to let you use it to get work if writing is where your interest lies. But there was some self-interest there, too," he allowed with a tilt of his head. "I figured he could help you get started without putting my story on every desk in town."

"Oh." She was still holding on to her elbows, but much of her tension had drained away into a glow she was afraid to name. Pride? "That was kind. Thank you." She licked her lips. "But please don't lie to me again. It's upsetting."

"Is it? I hadn't noticed," he said dryly.

She quirked a half smile at his facetious lie and dropped her gaze, realizing that she stood beside the bed. He was inside her room, hand on the latch of the door.

"I do appreciate all you're doing for me," she said sincerely. "It's hard to accept it, though. If I lash out, that's why. I don't like being something that has to be tolerated. Not again."

"You're not."

"You're not doing this out of friendship or affection, Travis." She wasn't being emotional about it. It was a fact. "It's obligation because we were once very briefly married. That's all."

He didn't contradict her and that was, perhaps, the most painful response he could have offered.

"I wouldn't help you if I didn't think you were worth the effort, Imogen."

As she stared at him, absorbing those words, her heartbeats slowed and grew so heavy they became a hammer, chipping away at her breastbone. "Do you mean that?"

"I do."

She nodded, unable to thank him because she was too moved. Her composure was crumbling.

"Do you mind?" she said in a strained voice. "I'm going to take my pills and get some sleep. The boss of my life says I have to."

He stood there a long moment before nodding once. He closed the door as he left.

She sat on the bed a long time, eyes closed, tears rolling down her cheeks.

# CHAPTER SIX

A FEW DAYS LATER, Travis booked them into the presidential suite in a Charleston mansion that had been converted to an exclusive boutique hotel. Their room had two floor-to-ceiling marble fireplaces, panels of Tiffany glass above the door frames, Italian chandeliers, a whirlpool tub in the bathroom and a twelve-foot Christmas tree in the lounge.

She was dying to say, "What, no piano?"

"I usually stay with my father, but his brothers and their wives are there, in town for the party."

"I'll try to make do," she murmured, noting there was a king bed and a daybed, along with a sofa here in the lounge that probably pulled out.

"You have an appointment at the spa. I'm seeing my barber and picking up my tuxedo."

"Okay." What else was she supposed to say? This was a play they were enacting. She had to report to hair and makeup, then say her lines without flubbing. "Is your father's party being held here?"

His mouth quirked. "A cruise of the harbor. I asked Gwyn to make all the arrangements and send the bills to me. She was going to book a paddle wheeler, but Vito's bank decided to buy a yacht to use for corporate events. He swears it was coincidence, but he likes to upstage me."

"Rivalries only matter when you're in second place. Someone said that to me recently." She circled a rivet in the upholstery of the chair she stood behind.

"You said it," he said dryly. "And when it comes to pleasing Gwyn, I'm forced to cede to Vito, so any sense of rivalry is pointless."

She smiled benignly, keeping her gaze on the chair. Lucky Gwyn.

"Are you all right? You've been quiet."

"Nervous," she admitted.

Suffering a hideous case of performance anxiety. After his kind words the other night, she had reminded herself not to let that affect her too deeply. To counteract any silly yearnings, she had counted up all the ways she could never rise to his level, which made for a depressing mood. She had decided to salvage some self-respect by repairing the damage she'd done, though. She would be the best fake wife he'd ever had.

Despite not having been a very good real one.

He left and she went down to the spa to let the proverbial birds and mice work their magic, massaging away her tension, painting her nails and pampering her skin, rolling her hair into fat twists of red-gold and lengthening her lashes to glamorous degrees.

When she returned to their room, she found a gown on the bed, this one in a rich amethyst. It didn't look as dramatic as the blue she'd brought with her, appearing quite plain and modest, but once she had it on, she saw its sensual elegance.

The draped back was so low, however, she couldn't wear a bra. That left her breasts thrusting against the sweep of velvet across her front. The cut of the skirt was narrow with a slit that rose nearly to her hip. Once she had her shoes on, she showed a lot of leg with each step.

She was swaying in front of her reflection, wondering who that red-carpet siren in the mirror was, when Travis returned.

He looked breathtaking in his tailored tuxedo. He was freshly shaved and his hair was trimmed into scrupulously perfect lines. And for once, in this single snapshot of time, with his compliment from the other night still floating like a love song in her ears, she was able to smile naturally as she looked on him, almost believing herself good enough for that ruthlessly handsome man.

Travis had walked into an electric fence as a kid— three wires he hadn't seen at summer camp because he'd been talking over his shoulder to a friend. The jolt had knocked him back so hard, he'd stumbled and landed on his butt.

That's how he felt as she smiled at him. Like he'd been chopped in the heart and the gut and the groin by a charge of something so strong, he came up short and had to catch himself on his back foot.

Dear God, she was a vision. He had known the color of that gown would accent the auburn and gold in her hair. He hadn't expected it to turn her eyes to emeralds and make her skin look delectable as whipped cream. The blue one from New York had been sexy on her, but he had taken one look at this dress on the mannequin and had known its simplicity would do her far more justice. It let Imogen shine through, from delicate shoulders to long limbs to the undeniable feminine mystique she possessed.

"You look beautiful." He felt something slipping from his grip and remembered why he'd run out. He offered the box. "I thought you might need jewelry."

"The rings?" Her smile fell away and her eyes widened enough to suggest panic. "No."

Her quick rejection was a fresh jolt, disturbing him. Why was she so adamant? Why did it sting that she didn't want to wear his rings?

"It's a necklace and earrings."

"Oh. On loan?" She was still wary.

"Yes."

"Okay, then." She came forward to take the box and opened it. "Thank you. They're lovely."

He watched her affix the earrings, thinking of her saying the night they went for dinner that he was only helping her out of obligation. Should he tell her that he'd spent a solid half hour choosing these for her, not because he was worried about how she looked, but because he wanted her to like them?

"Can you?" She lifted her hair so he could close the necklace.

He clasped the delicate chain and touched her shoulder, encouraging her to turn and face him again.

She smelled divine. He found his hand lingering on her shoulder, thumb lightly caressing the incredible softness of her skin. He barely resisted the desire to dip his head and taste her.

She shrugged and rubbed the spot where his hand had been, wiping away the goose bumps that had risen from her elbow up her arm. He wanted to rub them away himself, except he wanted to use a touch light enough to raise more. He wanted to draw her into his shirtfront and lick all the way up her throat until he was plundering the heat of her mouth.

"You're so beautiful. So sensual." His voice originated deep in his chest. "There couldn't have been only me." He hated the idea of her with another man. *Hated* it. But he couldn't blame her for it. Couldn't expect her to have been faithful to the vows he had made half-heartedly.

Her lashes flashed up, impossibly long and thick, making her look so innocent and vulnerable his insides ached. Shadows of hurt moved behind her gaze.

"You don't want me. What makes you think anyone else would?"

Until this moment, he hadn't believed she had been celibate. Now, as he saw how the breakdown of their marriage had only added to the rejections she had suffered from her father, battering her confidence into nothing, the truth impaled him.

She had denied herself sensual pleasure, not out of fidelity, but because she had been too hurt by him to risk another rebuff.

Remorse penetrated in a line from his throat to the middle of his chest, paralyzing him even as it stabbed excruciatingly deep.

"That's not true, Imogen." He took her arm again, feeling her stiffen at his touch, body already trying to pivot away from his. "I've said things to hurt you. Out of anger."

"I know." She closed her eyes, mouth not quite steady. "And it worked." She carefully removed her arm from his hand. Her eyes were glossed with tears as she looked at the door. "Can we not start a fight right now? I'm already worried how this will go."

"It will be fine."

She sent him a resigned look, as if she knew disaster was inevitable.

He didn't know how to convince her, though. How to repair the damage he'd done. With a nod, he moved to hold the door.

Imogen was doing well, *so well*. They had been among the last to board, tipping off Gwyn ahead of time to say they were running late so they could avoid the scrutiny of standing in the receiving line.

When Travis introduced her to his father on arrival, Henry was easily won over. It was painfully obvious he was dying for his son to marry and settle down.

Dark had fully fallen when the yacht left its mooring. The harbor was as still as a tub and the air crisp and clear under a fat moon and a blanket of stars.

Imogen felt as though she was an extra in a movie; everything was so perfect around her. The yacht was an elegant, ultramodern monstrosity with four decks, uncounted staterooms and an interior lounge of long sofas with a bar at one end. The whole thing was coated in holly and lights and wreaths and bows. On the outer deck off the stern, a small band from New Orleans played blues and jazz, Henry's favorite, apparently. They threw a few Christmas carols into the mix while the buffet dinner was served. Now people were starting to dance.

Most of the guests were in Henry's age bracket. They were curious enough about Travis's secret marriage and divorce to strike up conversations with them, but they confined their questions to an interest in where Imogen grew up and other nonthreatening topics.

Other guests were Travis's contemporaries, people he and Gwyn knew socially who also knew Henry. Some had worked for Henry during his years dominating the real estate markets in the Carolinas. They cast a few speculative looks toward Travis, but the South was known for its manners. Everyone was very civilized and the evening painless.

Until Imogen gaffed.

Of *course* she did. Of course it was *her*.

Gwyn was keeping Imogen firmly under her wing, giving her a rundown on who was who, frowning with distraction at a beautiful middle-aged woman who kept looking in their direction.

"She must be a plus-one. I don't recognize her. Do you remember her from the receiving line, Vito?" When her husband shook his head, she drew Travis from whatever thoughts had him drowning his gaze in his drink. "Who is that woman in the black-and-white dress, the one with the adorable pillbox hat?"

Travis glanced over, instantly arrested. "That would be my mother. You didn't invite her?"

"No." Gwyn's eyes widened in shock. "I've only seen one photo your father has of her when you were a baby. I'm sorry, but I can't even recall her name."

Now that Travis had noticed her, she approached. She was so much the beautiful feminine version of her son, it was uncanny. And she was younger than Imogen had expected. Her dark hair might have been colored to hide some gray, but it looked natural in its flawless chignon. Her skin was stunning, her makeup clever enough to take years off her already youthful appearance. Any woman of any age would be happy to have that figure.

"Travis, darling."

He stiffly allowed her to touch her cheek to his, then introduced them. Without being rude, Vito quickly excused himself and Gwyn to the dance floor, leaving Eliza Carmichael holding Imogen's hand with her ultrasoft, impeccably manicured and beautifully bejeweled fingers.

"How are you here?" Travis asked her.

"I came with Archie. Your father knew. He said he didn't mind."

"How long has that been going on?"

"Archie? It's a friendly date, not a romantic one. I wanted to see you. Meet Imogen." It was her clinging grip that got to Imogen. Eliza was cool and coiffed and smooth as silk, but there was something desperate in her hold on Imogen's hand. A plea.

"My son never tells me anything," she said, as if it was the oversight of a teenage boy neglecting to mention he'd asked a girl to prom. "I can't wait to get to know you properly."

"We have to mingle, Mother," Travis said flatly, running his hand along Imogen's arm until he had disengaged her from his mother's touch and could weave his fingers through hers himself.

Eliza barely flinched and her smile stayed pinned firmly in place. "Come for dinner tomorrow. Or any night while you're in town."

"We're at Dad's tomorrow and Christmas morning, flying back to New York right after. We're due in Hawaii by New Year's. It can't be changed."

Imogen hadn't known that "they" were going to

Hawaii, but that wasn't the issue right now. The issue was his mother was trying to reconcile with him and he was holding a grudge well past its expiration date.

"Why don't you come by our hotel for breakfast tomorrow?" Imogen suggested.

Travis's grip tightened, stretching the flesh between her fingers in warning.

"That would be lovely." Eliza held on to her Southern persona, warm without gushing, charming without being needy. "I'll look forward to that."

She moved away, but Travis was already tugging Imogen from the main cabin and down a hallway. What did they call them on boats? The passageway? It felt like a gangplank. He refrained from grabbing her by the ear or poking her spine with a sword point, but he was *mad*.

He ducked them into the first stateroom he found with an unlocked door, then snapped it closed and latched it behind them.

"Not your place, Imogen."

*Oh*, that got her back up. "Are you saying it is my place to put her in hers? I don't think so. And don't try to put me in mine. My instructions for this evening were to mind my manners. *You* were the one being rude when she only wants to spend a little time with you. That doesn't seem like an unreasonable request." What was wrong with him?

"It's called setting boundaries."

"Really? Because it looks like a refusal to forgive. You said she cheated on your father, not *you*. Your father was big enough to let her come to his party. Why are you angry about it? What's really going on?"

"Here's another boundary—don't try to get inside this. You know nothing about it."

"Does *she*? I've been on her side of that kind of hatred, Travis. It's not fair."

"Don't be so dramatic. I don't hate her. I see her on my terms, not hers and not *yours*."

"Why? What are you afraid of? That you might have to admit humans aren't perfect? You said you and she were alike. Was it so traumatic to see her mess up? Did it make you realize *you* could?"

"Take a step back, Imogen, because you are standing on my last nerve."

She was practically standing on his toes, chin hovering near the knot in his bow tie, genuinely angry on his mother's behalf. Being cut out like that was incredibly unfair. She knew exactly how that felt. From him, even.

"Fine. Don't spare her any of your precious minutes. I'll have coffee with her myself."

"You will not."

"What's the worst that can happen? You've never told me anything about yourself so I can't spill any of your secrets. All I can talk about is me and I don't reflect well in any of this, so your stellar reputation remains perfectly untarnished."

"I am warning you. *Do not* get involved."

"Oh, is your overactive need to control riled?" She poked him in the chest. She was that infuriated she just jabbed him right in the lapel, like pushing a button.

His hand shot up and grabbed her wrist. "My control is slipping by the second and you do *not* want to know what will happen when it's gone."

"What are you going to do? Kiss me into submission again? Prove that you can control me after all?

Go ahead, Travis. Go right the hell ahead." She knew it was a dare. Not to see if he would do it, but to hear him refuse to.

*I've said things to hurt you.*

Yes, he had. He'd said such hurtful things that she held her ground and dared him to say them again. To tell her he didn't want her. To *prove it.*

He swore in one explosive epithet. Then he dropped his mouth onto hers and she met him with her own pent-up anger. She thrust her hands into his hair and dragged him down and scraped her teeth across his bottom lip.

His arms banded around her and he crushed her tight to the pleats in his tuxedo shirt, fingers digging into her buttocks as he took control of the kiss and pivoted toward the bed.

The kiss changed on a dime, from anger to white-hot passion. His tongue dove into her mouth and she groaned as she greeted him, shuddering at the onslaught of sensations that accosted her—his familiar scent, his taste, his strength and the iron hardness behind his fly.

Then he was tilting them onto the bed, one hand stealing into the slit on her dress as they went. While he dragged his tongue down her throat, his palm claimed the heat between her thighs. He rocked his hand there until she was lifting into the motion, breathing, "Travis, please."

He rose enough to strip her panties down and throw them away, following the flow of the motion to drop off the edge of the mattress himself, onto his knees between her legs. He caught her thighs over his arms and grasped her hips, bringing her to the edge and his

waiting mouth. Her skirt rode up and a silent scream
gathered in her throat at the sudden, unavoidable, intimate contact. Ferocious, tingling heat flooded into
her loins, pulled and gathered there into a coil of tension by his unabashed attentions.

Why this? Why make her feel so exalted? So wor-
shipped and instantly swept away?

She arched herself to his pleasuring, hands claw-
ing at the blanket beneath her, head thrown back and
vision glazed by the rolling waves of arousal gathering strength as they radiated from her abdomen to her
limbs, drawing her toward a screaming pitch.

She wanted to beg, but couldn't even lick her lips.
Tension caught her up so quickly she could only pant
and gasp for air and finally drown in the swirling joy
of sudden, sweet release.

It wasn't enough, though. Even as her body pulsed
in a flood of ecstasy, she ached for more. For all of
him. Every inch of him covering her with his heat
and weight.

While he pulled away, making her whimper in loss.

For about one second, as he rose to his feet, she
thought he might have forced her into subjugation this
way. He looked down on her, limp and wanton, and
she knew he saw that she was utterly at his mercy. Her
heart stuttered and stalled, going into free fall.

Then he tore off his jacket, dropping it behind
him as he jerked open his pants, revealing his turgid
shape, hard and ready. His knees hit the edge of the
mattress, pushing hers further apart. He hooked his
hands under her arms, moved her up the bed, and then
his weight settled on her while the crest of his shape
pressed for entry.

She was slick and aching, taking him in one easy thrust that brought a sting of homecoming to her eyes. She managed to hook one bare thigh over his, but their clothing was tight and in the way, providing an erotic mix of textures and constriction when he began to thrust. His pants were a friction against her inner thighs, the hidden button of his shirt poked her breast, the silk of his bow tie grazed her jaw before he dipped his head and kissed her deeply, thrusting and thrusting, smooth and deep. Familiar and rough-sweet.

She was dimly aware this was earthy and wild, but it was also what she needed. Unabashed and fierce. Her body responded to his steady, determined possessiveness by twisting under waves of acute pleasure. When he tightened his hold on her so she felt the full measure and depth of his thrusts, she moaned with gratification, nearly coming apart with the rising tension. She gloried in how he made her feel, never wanting him to stop, but no human body could stand this level of hedonistic intensity.

She scraped her nails across the crisp back of his shirt, catching at the waist of his pants to pull him in tighter. Faster. More. *Now.*

White light seemed to flash behind her eyes, then she was falling. Gathered in with implosive energy, then expanding into all the dimensions ever created. Each piece of her took part of him with her so they reverberated together, shock wave after shock wave, disintegrating into all corners of the universe, together forever.

# CHAPTER SEVEN

HE COULD FEEL her twitching beneath him, still quaking with the final spasms of climax, breath still unsteady, but he was afraid to open his eyes and meet her gaze. That had been...

His mouth opened against her shoulder, a caress that made her moan and squeeze him with her intimate muscles, still reacting in latent pleasure to their collision.

Even so, his conscience was heavy. He'd been too rough. Too unrestrained. Not only that...

"I didn't use a condom," he said as he forced himself to extricate, rolling onto the bed next to her. The loss of her heat, her softness and elemental scent, nearly undid him. A growl of refusal to be denied locked in the base of his throat.

"Should I be worried?"

His heart lurched. "About disease? No." He had been a virgin of sorts for her tonight, having always worn condoms, even during their marriage. He had regular physicals, too, but... "Are you on the pill?"

"I'll take one of the morning-after kind."

A protest rose to his lips for no reason at all. He knew the precaution was for the best.

She sat up before he could decide what to say. Not even the sleeves of her dress were askew. When she stood to fetch her underpants and took her clutch into the bathroom, the only signs of their tussle were her ruffled hair and smudged lipstick.

He rose and straightened himself, locked in a kind of shock at how savagely they'd come together.

She emerged, makeup fixed, but pale and not meeting his gaze.

"Imogen." He put out a hand and she halted beyond his reach, something in her stiffness keeping him from moving close enough to touch her. "Are you all right?"

"Of course." She lifted her lashes, but her expression was the cautious one of supreme cooperation, like he'd seen after he had kissed her at the boutique. The one where she fell into line out of sheer defensiveness. His heart lurched.

"We don't want anyone to know. We should go back out." She veered around his outstretched hand and unlocked the door, glancing back before leaving without him.

He lingered, reached to straighten the blanket and hated himself a little more for erasing that small bit of evidence, when he would rather hang on to their moment of passion with both hands.

*You don't want me. What makes you think anyone else would?*

He had been astonished when she had said it. He could remember being astounded that she really had been a virgin on their wedding night. She had been so sensual and responsive, reacting to his lightest touch. She had said something at the time about dating in the wrong pool, not the sort of men she found truly attractive. He remembered being curious but not asking questions, because he was smart enough to know that sexual pasts were never good topics with current lovers.

His own past seemed tawdry against her standards, especially when he'd left her thinking he didn't want her.

*I've said things to hurt you.*

*And it worked.*

He'd been fearful he'd killed whatever she'd once felt for him when she had said that. He'd spent the evening sick with himself for kicking over what had actually been quite precious, long before he realized its value.

At the same time, he'd been fighting jealousy. He had no right to such a thing, but even Vito's eyes had lit with surprised appreciation at the sight of Imogen tonight and he was 10,000 percent devoted to Gwyn. Everyone was looking at Imogen, not because she was Travis's surprise ex-wife, but because she was that entrancing.

He was proud to stand beside her, but threatened. He wanted her, but so did everyone else. And there was nothing that gave him a claim on her except maybe obligation on her part for the help he was offering her.

All of that had been whirling in him as his mother showed up to act as any mother would on meeting the woman who might have been her daughter-in-law.

His mother's presence had reminded him that any sort of monogamy was an exercise in futility. It didn't matter how much he wanted Imogen. He couldn't have her. Not forever. Not in a way he could believe in.

The pressure had reached a boiling point in him.

Imogen getting cozy with his mother had been his snapping point.

He wasn't still punishing his mother. He wasn't that small. But the accusations Imogen had been throwing at him about being human had been all too accurate when primal forces had been taking him over. Then she had dared him to kiss her.

He hadn't been trying to control her. He'd barely been able to control any of that—which was a terrifying admission to make to himself. But the second he had touched her, he hadn't been thinking of anything at all. Nothing except pleasure. Ensuring hers, then enjoying his.

*We don't want anyone to know.*

He supposed that was for his benefit. She had pulled herself together and was out there putting on a brave face to protect his reputation, and all he wanted to do was go out and manacle her wrist with a firm grip, telling the entire guest list, "She's mine."

He wanted to drag her back in here and prove it again. And again and again.

The instinct, so base on the heels of acting like such a caveman, left him shaken. He splashed cold water on his face and pulled himself together.

When he finally returned to the party, he didn't spot her right away. The delay was just long enough for a knee of panic to kick into his abdomen. Then he found her outside, at the rail with his father.

He noted the wrinkles pressed into the velvet of her dress. Anyone else would imagine they had been caused by her sitting down for a few minutes, but he knew his own weight had imprinted those lines into her gown. He burned with primitive satisfaction as he approached. Burned in the sinful fires of wanting to do it again.

As he came up behind them, he heard his father offering a history lesson, pointing to heritage properties barely visible in the dark.

Unable and unwilling to go another second without touching her, he found her waist with his splayed hand. "Dance?"

She turned, revealing a brief flash of pain that nearly knocked Travis over the rail and into the water before she swept her lashes low, leaving an impression of having been chastised.

"If you'd like. Excuse me, Henry."

"You two have fun," his father said with an indulgent smile.

His father's pleasure against her wariness set Travis's heart on its edge. He took her into his embrace, but she felt stiff and awkward.

"He was only telling me about some buildings. It wasn't anything about you or us." The pang in her voice rang like a bell deep in his ears, sending painful echoes into his chest.

"I wasn't trying to cut that short." Maybe he was. What point was there in letting his father get to know her? He'd dropped by the house today with a half-assed explanation, which his father had only absorbed with a pained nod.

*Forgive me for hoping your reasons for divorce weren't as insurmountable as mine with your mother. Of course, if I was still married to your mother, I wouldn't have Gwyn and her children, would I? I guess these things work out as they're meant to.*

Was that his father's idea of something "working

out"? His first wife had cheated and his second had been diagnosed months after their wedding day, gone within a couple of pain-filled years.

Imogen's hand in his felt tense. All of her did. He was shoving a mannequin around the dance floor.

She had her chin tucked, hiding her expression. When he looked around to see if anyone had noticed, he caught Gwyn frowning at them with concern.

He drew Imogen toward the rail, where a shadow was cast by the bulkhead. "Imogen, I'm—"

"Don't say you're sorry. You'll make it worse." She kept her face turned toward the water, so the guests couldn't see she had a sheen of misery on her eyes.

"I hurt you." A cloud of remorse choked him. He sidestepped to shield her with his body and tried to enfold her, somehow thinking if he held her gently now, it would erase his fervent embrace from before.

"I hurt myself. I thought I was proving something, but now there's just one more thing to worry about. And for what? Nothing changes." She pushed away and pressed herself to the rail, looking up to hold back tears. He watched her visibly gather her composure, taking breaths to steady her shoulders and calm her profile.

"Are you two all right? Did your mother say something?" Gwyn appeared beside them, looking to him with concern.

Travis bit back a curse while Imogen quickly found a bright smile.

"I'm a little seasick. Please don't say anything." She squeezed Gwyn's arm. "You know what sort of rumor that will start. But maybe fetch me a ginger ale?" she asked Travis.

So quick with the lies it was terrifying, making the other thing she'd said a harsh truth: nothing had been changed by their lovemaking.

He went to order her drink, thinking he would never again attend a party on a boat. There was no escape when the seas grew rough.

Imogen's cheeks ached from the strain of holding a fake smile. Her shoulders were carved marble, her molars practically shaved down to nothing after grinding them to endure this interminable night.

It was after midnight, yet somehow the hotel concierge had come through for her and made a purchase from an all-night pharmacy, leaving her package next to the bathroom sink as she had asked in her brief call from the ladies' room aboard the yacht.

"Oh, for heaven's sake!" she cried as she read the directions. "Is nothing in this life simple?" Marching out of the bathroom, she found Travis unraveling his tie and pulling it from his collar. His jacket already hung off the back of a chair.

He stalled with surprise. "What's wrong?"

"Can you look up if these interact? There's no point taking both if one cancels out the other." She shoved the contraceptive and the antibiotics at him, then went straight back to the bathroom to remove her makeup, so overwhelmed and frustrated she was shaking.

She was still reacting to their impetuous lovemaking, not quite believing it had happened. After his claim that he'd only said things in the past to hurt her, implying they hadn't all been true, she had had a perverse need to test his desire. As they fought, she had goaded him. Part of her was thrilled to discover they were as explosive as they'd been during their marriage. But as physically exciting and satisfying as their lovemaking had been, all she'd learned was that he was capable of having sex with someone he disliked.

How devastating.

He came in to set both items beside her on the vanity. "They're fine."

She finished brushing her teeth, poured herself a glass of water and took her medication. Then she dropped the contraceptive into her palm and threw it into her mouth, right there where he could watch her take it and there wouldn't be any accusations later if things went awry.

He inhaled sharply, as though her action was a bludgeon that landed someplace very mortal and damaging to him.

"No discussion, then," he said in a strained voice.

"What's to discuss?" she asked after washing it down. "You don't want a baby with me. You're already sorry you even touched me. Do you mind?" She lifted her hair and turned her back so he could remove the necklace.

He slid the pendant free and set it on the vanity with a muted shower of gold links against marble. Then he surprised her by taking hold of her hips. The weight of his head came to rest against the crook of her neck and shoulder. The heat of his forehead almost thawed the rigidity gathered there.

"My only regret is that I didn't treat you more gently. You destroy me, Imogen." His voice was grim, but his breath feathered against the top of her spine. "When I'm with you like that, nothing matters. You're like a drug."

Damaging and ugly. Her heart skittered and swirled down a drain. "And you hate it. Hate me. *I know.*"

"I don't hate you." His hands tightened. "I don't hate how we are together. That is the problem!"

She shakily took off the earrings, but he didn't release her. His body heat and the press of his mouth on her hair remained while she set aside the earrings. She stared at their hooked shape against the marble, unwilling to lift her gaze to the mirror and see herself in his odd embrace. She stood in his hold as though his body was a compress, something that eased the ache while the injury remained.

His breath wafted against her skin again. His hands massaged gently on her hips.

"You're so fierce and dangerous to me, I forget that you're slight and tender and bruise easily."

"I'm fine. We had quickies before. If I wasn't into it, I would have told you."

He drew a deeper breath as he lifted his head, but when he released his grip on her hips, he folded his arms across her front, gathering her into him.

She felt so safe in that moment, with her one arm resting over his at her waist, her other hand catching at his strong wrist where his arm banded her collarbone, she let herself lean into him and close her eyes. His cheek rested against her head, lips near her ear. She felt the light kiss he placed there and nearly wept at the sweetness of it.

"I'm tired of the hurt and the blame and the guilt," she confessed in a whisper. "I'm tired of being a disappointment."

"You're not."

She drew away and turned to face him. "You don't want this. You don't want *me*."

His lips tightened into a grim line and he looked away, not at his reflection but in the other direction, as if he couldn't look at himself right then, either.

"I don't want to be at the mercy of the way you make me feel. You have always been too much for me. Never not enough. I don't know how to deal with the force that is Imogen. You're so beautiful and passionate. I make rash promises I can't keep, just for the privilege of touching you. I want you more than I can bear."

"I don't want to be your self-destructive impulse, Travis. I want…"

She wanted him to love her. To want her forever. Those had been her thoughts the first time, when she had been young and idealistic and had succumbed within a week to blind passion. She had saved herself for her husband because she had believed if a man married her, it would mean he loved her.

She was older and wiser now, but… "I want you to like me," she said shakily. "At least a little. I know I can't look to any man to complete me, but we ought to offer each other something besides orgasms. A lifetime commitment was an unrealistic expectation for both of us. I know that. We should have had an affair four years ago, but an affair now is madness. You resent me. I'm a charity case. It's too unequal."

"It's not charity. I'm helping you because I want to, Imogen. Because I *care*. I wouldn't forgive myself if I didn't." He set his hand against the side of her neck and looked her in the eyes.

*I care.* Silly, foolish hope began to thrum like a trapped bird in her chest.

"But trust is an issue for me." His thumb stroked against her throat. "That's not all on you. I didn't trust you when we married and I didn't yet have a reason *not* to."

"Then I lived up to your lowest expectations," she muttered.

"How much did you trust me?" he challenged quietly.

"You didn't *ask*."

"Fair enough." He acknowledged that with a tilt of his head. "But this *is* an opportunity for the affair we should have had. One without added pressures like marriage or ulterior motives."

"One without expectations of any kind? Not even a future?" She said the words so they both understood the rules, even though it was a heel on her heart.

"Yes."

That wasn't such a terrible thing. He did care for her in his way and the surrender of defenses and weapons between them would bring an approximation of the peace she desperately longed for. It was something.

Covering his hand, she turned her head so she could kiss the inside of his wrist.

His breath shuddered as he drew her in. She lifted her mouth for the press of his and it was pure magic. All the charged emotions flipped and became a magnetism, strong and electric, sealing them into rightness. His kiss was urgent but tender. Passionate but sweet. So, so sweet.

They stood there a long time, hands whispering across clothing as they kissed. She ran her fingers through his hair again and again, loving the short, spiky strands, so dearly familiar. He cupped her butt and took soft bites down the side of her throat, laughing with satisfaction when he made her shiver and moan.

"Still my fatal weakness," she said sheepishly, shrugging and drawing back to rub the lingering tingles.

"I'm going after the small of your back before we're done," he promised in a voice that hit like a velvet punch in her midsection. His fingertips tickled into those delicate hollows that took out her knees.

As she let him take her weight, she looked into the expression that convinced her she was someone worth the trouble, the one that was fierce and possessive, lit with approval and hunger and abject desire, all his attention on her. It was intoxicating to be looked at like that. This was why she had fallen for him the first time.

Closing her eyes so she wouldn't start to believe in the impossible, she ran her hands up behind his neck, reveling in the luxury to do so, and drew him down for another kiss.

He dipped and caught her behind the knees, carrying her to the bedroom where he set her on her feet by the bed. When he started to kiss her, she drew back a half step.

"I want to look at you," she told him shyly and started to search for the buttons in the pleats on his shirt. "Feel you."

He yanked at his shirt, pulling it from his waistband and rending the buttons to get it open before stripping it with a powerful twist of his tanned shoulders. When one cuff hung up at his wrist, he swore like he meant it, making her laugh.

"We have all night," she pointed out.

"You don't understand how badly I want to be naked

with you," he growled, making her laugh again as the shirt got trampled so he could jerk his arm free. Then he shed his pants and underwear in one swift move.

He straightened and all of her melted at the sight of this man. The handful of years had added muscle to his chest and seemed to broaden his shoulders. The taper to his flat abdomen and narrow hips was accentuated and sexier than ever. He was starkly aroused, flesh thrusting with desire atop the tense columns of his thighs.

As intimidating as he was, however, so broad and aggressive-looking, his hands were surprisingly gentle as he drew the dress down her shoulders. It fell to her elbows and the bodice drooped, exposing her breasts.

Her nipples, already hard points, pinched even tighter as he looked at her like he'd uncovered a treasure, seemingly having forgotten himself as his breath became audible and unsteady.

He lightly guided her hands down to her sides, so the dress continued its fall. It puddled around her feet, leaving her standing in only her midnight blue thong and a pair of high heels in black velvet with a velvet ribbon tied in a bow at each ankle.

The hiss of his breath deepened as his gaze took her in, crossing from shoulder to shoulder, singeing her quivering breasts and making her stomach suck in. Heat flooded into her loins, dampening the thong he lightly traced with the tip of his finger. Her thighs trembled in reaction to his touch, making her feel unsteady in her shoes.

Very slowly, excruciatingly slowly, he eased her thong down, exposing her inch by inch, making her clench in anticipation and bite her lip at the tease of it.

"Don't close your legs. Let them fall."

"Travis," she breathed, tortured.

"I know. I want you, too. But let me look." The lace finally fell down her legs, but that only left her helpless to the torment of his light caress. He traced and teased and had her moaning under the tickling touch that only incited, didn't assuage.

She reached to take him in hand, squeezing a message of what she needed from him. He grunted out a harsh curse and thrust into her grip, then caught her against him so the impact of hot skin against her own made her cry out.

They kissed then, madly and deeply. Without restraint. Wet and hot and with such lust she thought she would combust. She rubbed herself against him, needing the scrape of chest hair against her nipples, and lifted her knee against his hip, longing for the shape that stroked her sensitive flesh to invade and satisfy her.

Suddenly she was on her back, his big body over her, his hand cradling her jaw as he looked into her eyes.

"I'm supposed to be doing this properly." He found a condom and applied it.

"I can't wait." She hurried him, guiding him to where she wanted him.

He rolled, pulling her atop him. "Take what you want," he said grittily. "Then I'll do it my way."

She rose on her knees to impale herself, riding him to a swift peak, breasts teased by his wicked hands the whole way. But she was hungry, hungry, hungry and kept moving even as she was shuddering and lost in the ecstasy of climax. She wanted to gorge herself on him and kept going until she was clenched in the vise of orgasm a second time, this one even stronger and more satisfying than the first.

Only then did she melt onto him, all his hard muscle a hot ceramic containing explosive chemicals.

"Thank you," she murmured as she splayed herself on him.

"Oh, no, my beauty. That was for me and it was amazing. Now, though, now I'll give you something to be thankful for." He rolled so she was beneath him again, then slid away to kiss and nibble and lick, all the way down her front. He sucked at her nipples in turn, taking his time, and sighed his hot breath across her navel before threatening a bite of each hip and blew softly across her mound.

She writhed on the covers and her heel caught. He made a noise of sympathy, as if she was injured, and rose to his knees. He took off her shoes with great care, pressing his mouth to her ankles and biting gently against her calf. His fingertips teased behind her knees and he scraped his stubble against her inner thigh.

As the heat of anticipation built in her core, he sent her a wicked smile and rolled her over. His teeth nipped her buttock and his mouth opened in her lower back, the nerve bundles there so sensitized to his caress that she cried out, while goose bumps raced across her whole body and heat flooded into her buttocks and loins.

With a firm touch, he parted her thighs, making her gasp at the audacity of it. Then he was toying with her moist folds while pressing kisses to her back. Her scalp tingled and she couldn't speak, she was held in such a paroxysm of pleasure.

"I could do this forever," he said hotly against her nape. "Touch you, taste you." He settled over her, hot shaft branding the crease of her buttocks.

For long minutes, he braced himself over her like that, shifting and letting her feel his weight, his hot skin, imprinting his scent on her like an animal. Maybe it was a move of dominance, but it felt like something else. None of that strength and power was meant to hurt her, he seemed to be saying. He was reminding her she could trust him.

Her hips lifted of their own accord.

When he rose enough to let her roll onto her back and kissed her tenderly, she opened like a blossom, taking him between her legs, accepting the length of him with one smooth sink of his hips against hers.

She was lost in the miasma of sexual bliss, then. Caressing him, moaning with joy at each thrust, licking into his mouth, holding nothing back. Offering herself without reserve.

"Look at me." He stopped moving to smooth her hair from her perspiration-soaked temple.

She could hardly open her eyes. When she did, the intimacy was almost too much to bear. He held her on a precipice so fine and sharp she was ready to scream, body pulsing and aching for release.

His eyes glowed with fierce possessiveness. He knew he held her in the very palm of his hand, all of her given over to him without conditions. His voice was drugged and smoky, hypnotic.

"It's time. Come with me now."

He began to move in heavy, purposeful thrusts. A fresh wave of pleasure, mightier and more all-encompassing, engulfed her. As it broke and curled over her, he shouted his culmination.

They tumbled to the bottom, clinging to the other as the world shattered around them.

The phone jangled her from a deep sleep, making her gasp awake to the realization she was not alone in bed.

Travis was spooned so tightly to her, her skin pulled painfully as he shifted to reach past her and pick up the receiver before it could ring again.

"Sanders." His voice was gritty and sensual enough to curl her toes.

They'd done their best to rewrite the Kama Sutra last night, then fell asleep wrapped around each other. It had been greedy and gratifying, conversation limited to what they liked and wanted. She felt like she was his again, the way she had when they'd been married. His lover, his wife, his woman.

*Careful, Imogen.*

Whoever was on the line was female. Imogen didn't try to make out what she was saying. She was caught between a desire to fall back asleep and put off facing reality, and a flood of sensual memory that made her want to squiggle her butt into Travis's growing arousal.

She was tired and achy, but still bathed in sexual satisfaction, wanting only to snuggle back into his arms and stay there.

"We'll see you then." He hung up and let his hand land on her hip in a light smack that was cushioned by the covers. "Mother will be downstairs in thirty minutes."

"Okay, you were right. Breakfast was a dumb idea,"

she conceded, pulling the sheet over her head. "Enjoy your I-told-you-so."

He didn't say anything and didn't move. His hand was still resting on her hip and his chest grazed her back. He didn't even nudge himself against her butt, just let his swelling sex rest against the softness of her cheeks.

"Are you mad?" she asked.

"I'd rather stay in bed, so, yeah. I'm put out."

She lowered the sheet and made herself look at him.

Here was the man she had fallen so hard for, undeniably masculine with his stubble and short, spiky lashes and that air of smug animal pride as his gaze hung up on her mouth.

"Or are you asking if I'm mad that you put out? Hell, no. Last night was fantastic."

"Nice." She jabbed her elbow into his chest.

He captured her beneath him and gave one warning scrape of his stubbled chin against her smooth one, then planted a firm kiss on her lips.

"Shower," he declared, shoving himself off her and dragging most of the covers with him so they fell off the side and onto the floor. "Separately, or we won't leave this room for a week." He walked naked into the bathroom.

Travis wasn't carrying a grudge against his mother, despite what Imogen had accused last night. He had been angry when her infidelity was exposed. Of course he was. One minute, his family life had been stable and his parents' marriage—to his eyes—had been loving. Then overnight his mother's cheating had come to light and everything had blown up.

She'd moved out and all the little ways she had run their lives, things that Travis had taken for granted, were over. He'd not only had to take responsibility for himself, but his father had been a wreck, turning to the bottle in a way so distressing, Travis had worried about leaving him alone while he was at school.

As a result, he had resisted leaving his father to visit his mother, only going when he absolutely had to. She'd been living with her new lover anyway, so it had been beyond uncomfortable to join her. He'd been old enough to decide where he went and for how long and, yes, he had probably been punishing her by avoiding her.

The distance in their relationship had stuck through his last years of high school. When he left for university, he had developed a full enough life; he simply didn't have time for anything but his own ambitions. He'd checked in with his father quite often, but only because Henry had taken up with his office janitor, Gwyn's mom. It had been a strange enough romance he'd wanted to keep an eye on it, but mending fences with his own mother hadn't been a priority. Once his career had started in earnest and he moved to New York, he'd made do with calling her a few times a year.

Had her actions in his impressionable teen years left him thinking all women were inconstant? Perhaps. It was certainly another reason he'd been convinced his marriage to Imogen was unlikely to last.

Did he hate and blame his mother for that? Want to punish her for it? No. They simply didn't have a lot to talk about.

But as he sat down with her, he noticed for the first time in more than a decade that she was aging. There were lines cut into her natural beauty. He wondered uncomfortably if Imogen was right. Maybe he'd been unfair to Eliza, avoiding her this long.

He let Imogen carry the conversation, even though there was a certain danger in letting her speak for them as a couple. He was especially conflicted because he'd spent the last several hours trying to meld their bodies into one. They *were* a couple, but a temporary one.

That word *temporary* caused a tightness in him he didn't want to examine.

The women wound down from their agreeable comments on what a nice party it had been, how the weather had cooperated and what a versatile and accommodating band had been found for the occasion.

His mother cut him a wary glance before broaching the real purpose of their meeting. "I didn't even know Travis had been married."

"No one did," Imogen assured her with a sheepish wrinkle of her nose. "We were young. I was *very* young. Just turned twenty. No one should embark on a lifetime commitment before they're twenty-five, if you want my older and wiser opinion."

"How old are you now?"

"Twenty-four," Imogen said cheekily.

His mother's mouth trembled between a rueful smile and something more delicately pointed. When she spoke, he thought it might be more for his benefit than Imogen's. "Perhaps that's why my marriage didn't work. That, and the age difference between us."

Travis narrowed his eyes, tempted to dismiss it as his mother taking advantage of the situation to make excuses for her behavior, but even though he knew full well she was eighteen years younger than his father, he had never stood back and examined that gap in the context of how it might have affected their marriage.

"Was Henry as ambitious as Travis?" Imogen asked. "I found that part hard. I was trying to do my own thing, having zero success, while he was knocking it out of the park." Imogen touched his arm. "I don't say that as blame. I was excited for you, but with things as they were with Dad, I found it hard to watch you excel at every turn while I was stuck in one place."

He had stopped asking Imogen about her work when she had said very tersely that her father had had to cut her piece on him. At the time, her lack of explanations had awakened his suspicions that she had interviewed him to ensnare him. He'd decided she wasn't being completely honest with him and, as it turned out, she *had* been hiding something, just not what he had imagined.

"Henry was a very big deal," his mother was saying with a wistful sort of awe. "People were begging him to go into politics. We used to joke that I was his trophy wife." Her humor turned more poignant. "In some ways, I was. He was at a point in his life he was ready for a brood of children, but he was so busy conquering the landscape he rarely had time for the son he had. I found motherhood quite overwhelming and tried to be happy as a homemaker, supporting Henry, but I felt as though my best years were passing me by." She glanced at Travis again, pleading for understanding. "I didn't *lack* ambition. I hadn't had a chance to fulfill it."

Travis looked into his coffee. His mother had gone on to open a string of boutiques, doing quite well for herself. She had never asked for his help with it. Aside from the odd job around the house, she'd never asked him for anything.

"I felt quite isolated while Henry was pulled in so many directions. It was hard to believe he loved me when his attention was never *on* me. It wasn't until I'd hurt him so badly he couldn't forgive me that I realized how deep his feelings really were."

"But he's forgiven you," Imogen hurried to say. "You were dancing last night. I saw you. It was lovely to watch. You moved well together."

His mother smiled, but it didn't reach her eyes. She was still looking at Travis, gauging his reaction. Seeking a capitulation of sorts from him.

"Infidelity is a deal breaker. If all we'd had wrong between us was my immaturity, I would try again, even this late in the day." Her voice was a little stronger, carrying the tone of maternal wisdom one ignored at their own peril.

An acquaintance approached their table, forcing them to change the subject, and the rest of the meal passed innocuously. Toward the end, however, Imogen seemed to deliberately excuse herself to the powder room, leaving him to have a private word with his mother.

"I like her," she said with a warm smile.

When he didn't say anything, her smile faded.

"Travis, if it's my fault you can't open your heart—"

"It's not," he cut in. Maybe her actions had colored the way he had approached his marriage, contributing to its failure, but… "I don't understand what marriage is even for," he stated with acerbic challenge. "Don't say 'children' when you just told me you felt held back by motherhood. It's not a lifetime commitment. We've both proven that's not true. So why bother with it? It's a social construct that serves no purpose." He set down his mug. His coffee left a bitter taste in the back of his throat.

She was taken aback, blinking once, twice, then said with faint astonishment, "I wasn't talking about marriage. I was talking about love."

"Also temporary," he stated flatly. If such a thing existed at all.

His mother gasped a protest, but she had stepped out on his father because she hadn't believed he loved her. He had, but not enough to keep her faithful. His father had gone on to love someone else, proving Travis's point that the heart was fickle.

Imogen might not be as self-interested and bloodless as he'd thought her, but she hadn't loved him when they married. Not enough to be honest with him. She didn't love him now.

They were finding common ground, though, and he didn't want that jeopardized.

"We're in a good place, Mother. Don't mess with it."

"Are you?" she asked stiffly. "Your father thought that about us and look how that turned out."

Imogen returned to find Travis glaring at his mother, not nearly in the space of reconciliation she had hoped to see between them. It left her feeling defensive for forcing the meeting. Now they had to pack up and move to Henry's for Christmas Eve and morning.

At least the children provided a buffer and a distraction. It wasn't until they had been put down for the night that things became a little awkward.

Vito was liberally pouring wine with his family's

label and they were all sitting around the winking tree, mellow after a lovely dinner, when Gwyn asked Imogen if she was missing out on celebrating with her own family.

"No one left." She explained that she had lost her mother and sister quite young and her father this year.

"Your first Christmas without him. I'm so sorry."

"We didn't celebrate," she dismissed easily. "This has been really lovely. Thank you for including me."

They all looked at her the way other people did when she said she didn't celebrate, like they were trying to tell if it was a religious choice or something.

"Not at all?" Gwyn asked.

"I put up a tree a few times, but…" She shrugged off how futile that had been, sipping her wine, aware of Travis staring at her.

When they went to bed a short while later, he said, "Your father didn't even give you Christmas gifts?"

She paused in undressing. "Please don't spoil what's been a really nice evening." She stepped out of her skirt and folded it lengthwise, adding with some anxiety, "And please don't feel like you have to surprise me with a gift tomorrow to make up for that. It would upset me."

"Why?"

"Because it would be charity."

He took her into his arms, making it impossible for her to keep unbuttoning her blouse. "I hate him, you know."

"*Please* don't waste your energy."

"If you insist."

He kissed her and made love to her tenderly, then woke her with a coffee topped with whipped cream and sprinkled with chocolate shavings.

"The minion is awake and begging to open her gifts. Do you want to open this here or downstairs?" He set her coffee on the night table and held out a small box wrapped in gold with a glittering ribbon.

"I told you—" She sat up to admonish him.

"They looked so good on you, I kept them. I was going to give it to you anyway." He dabbed his finger on her whipped cream and touched it to her nose. "Say 'thank you.'"

"Really?" She rubbed it away with the back of her wrist, but her avaricious fingers were already closing on the box, itching to tear it open. He had insanely good taste in jewelry and she was already grieving the loss after giving back last night's pendant and earrings. They were so pretty.

"Yes, really. Merry Christmas."

For the first time in more than a dozen years, it was. As emotion clogged up her throat, turning her voice husky, she leaned forward to kiss him. "Thank you."

Imogen had spent the last four years blaming herself for the breakdown of their marriage. Travis had been so disparaging in their final conversations, first angry about the credit card, then agreeing immediately that, yes, divorce was a great idea. She had been convinced she'd brought nothing to their relationship.

By the time she'd had a lawyer request the settlement Travis had promised in their prenup, he'd barely been speaking to her. She'd felt small and rejected, unworthy of his love in the first place. It was hardly a surprise he hadn't wanted to stay married to her. Given her relationship with her father at the time, it had been her default to take the blame for Travis not being in love with her.

Their two days of truce and lovemaking and pleasant visiting with his family reminded her why she had fallen for him in the first place. He was wicked smart, keeping up with Vito on investment-banking talk long after her eyes had crossed, but always listened to her opinion even when it turned into a spirited debate. He was a gentleman and, yes, a neat freak, but it was kind of nice that he hung her coat and wiped a bit of flour from her cheek.

And seeing him with his niece and nephew was another side of him altogether, the kind of thing that made a woman's ovaries burst into flower.

She had to keep her expectations realistic, however. It was a point driven home to her when he screwed in his earbuds to watch some work-related slide show on his laptop during their flight back to New York, then made phone calls in the car all the way into the city.

She wasn't so much stung by it as sad. Was it ambition that drove him to shut her out? Or was it a kind of rebound after their closeness the last couple of days? Was she too much for him, as he had claimed that first night in Charleston? How was that any better than not being enough?

*I make rash promises I can't keep, just for the privilege of touching you.*

She had to remember he wasn't making any promises at all this time. She had to be careful not to imagine he was. Figuring out how to protect herself from heartbreak was a challenge, though, when she was so susceptible to him, feeling his withdrawal so keenly.

"Did you hear me?" he asked, touching her arm.

She had wandered onto the terrace of his building after they arrived back, hugging herself, lost in thought.

"Hmm? Oh, okay." Her breath fogged as she spoke and she nodded, then admitted as his words penetrated, "No. I don't know what you said."

"I have to run to the office." He gave her a look of amusement. "Where were you?"

"Thinking about making a doctor's appointment." As far as protecting herself went, that was a good start.

He frowned. "Did the flight hurt your ear?"

"No. I want to go on birth control."

"I wear—" he started to say, then made a face as he recalled his slip. "Probably a good idea. Thank you." Something enigmatic passed over his expression. He seemed to shake off whatever he was thinking with a distracted nod. "Let me know when you have to be there. I'll arrange the car."

"Thank you. Do you want me to cook tonight?"

"You don't have to."

"I'll see you when I see you, then, and make do with whatever is in the fridge." She set her hands on his chest, preparing to rise on tiptoe to kiss him goodbye.

He tucked his chin. "I meant we can go out for dinner if you'd rather. I'll only be gone an hour."

"Right." She patted his chest. "I've played that game before. I'll see you when I see you," she repeated with good-natured rue and stretched to peck his cheek.

His hands closed on her arms, keeping her from retreating after her kiss. "That sounds like a reprimand."

"Not at all. You have even more demands on your time than you used to. I occupy an even smaller slice of your life than I did then. I accept that." At least, she was trying to. "I'll use the time to look for work. Rowan emailed me. It sounds like she might have something. I have to read it properly."

Nic showed me your piece on Travis. I hope you don't mind. I'd love to know what you would do with my mother's story, given the chance.

Imogen wasn't taking it seriously, but writing a proposal was a good exercise.

He dropped his touch and stuffed his hands in his pockets.

"What you said to my mother… Four years ago was a very busy time for me, expanding, taking on projects that were bigger than anything I'd attempted before. I had no idea what was going on with your father. You're right that I didn't ask, but even so, I wasn't trying to diminish you when I put work ahead of spending time with you."

"I know. And I don't expect you to make me a priority now." She smiled, but her voice felt stuck like a wishbone lodged in her chest and she couldn't resist saying, "But I feel for your mother. This is very different. You and I aren't married and I don't have a child with you, but she did. It must have hurt when your father shut her out. I just wish you and she were on better terms."

"It's not that easy," he muttered, swiveling away to stare grimly at the view. "When I told you that Dad drank after she was gone, I meant he dove into a bottle and didn't come out. He's a teetotaler now, but it was *bad*. I was still in high school, but I was suddenly the parent, getting him to bed, getting him to work. I couldn't leave him alone and go stay with her. I was scared of what he might do to himself. That's why I didn't see her."

"Wasn't there anyone to help? What about your uncles?"

He shook that off. "Dad wouldn't even admit Mother was gone or why, let alone that he couldn't cope. His business was suffering. That's why I had to keep such a sharp eye on things. I don't blame her for his drinking, but I couldn't abandon him when *she* just had. She and I grew apart for all of those reasons." His profile was like granite. "I can't pretend everything is fine with her after that."

Fair enough, she supposed. "How long did it go on? His drinking? I mean, he seemed fine the other night…"

"He's been sober for years. He started going to meetings when I was leaving for university. I genuinely wasn't sure I'd be able to go, but he was really trying, pulling himself together. Then I found out it was because he was seeing Gwyn's mom. She was the janitor in his office. I didn't know what to think of that. I was suspicious and programmed to be protective of Dad. When I did have time to go home, it was to check on him. I wasn't choosing him over my mother.

"I'm not still nursing anger. Well, she said some things the other day that annoyed me, but if she was sick or in trouble, if she really needed me, of course I would be there for her. But on a day-to-day basis, all we have is nostalgia and I'm not a particularly sentimental person."

That was a warning, she was sure. She looked to her feet.

"Was she good for him in the end? Gwyn's mom, I mean."

"He would say so," Travis said with an impatient shrug. "But she got sick almost right away. He spent most of their marriage taking her to treatment and was shattered when she died. Fortunately, Gwyn was there, giving him someone to stay sober for, checking on him often enough I was able to move to New York, but..."

But none of that added up to a good reason to become attached to anyone. She wondered if he had any positive experiences with love. Even his stepsister had been through a rough time that had left nuclear fallout all over him.

"Were you worried about your dad when we were married?"

"I'm always worried about him," he said with a grimace. "One of my coping strategies is to bury myself in work. I'll cop to that." He sent her a look of frustration, one that made her think he might be regretting all he had just revealed. "I did push work between us when we were married. I had set myself some lofty goals and my desire to spend time with you was a threat to them. Today it's the other way around, though." His voice softened. "I'm trying to clear up a few things so we can have more downtime in Hawaii."

"Really?" She was genuinely astonished, but touched. "You want to walk the beach and hold hands at sunset?" It was a tease, but also a tantalizing idea. A wish.

"Among other things," he said, mouth quirking, but he lifted her hand and kissed her knuckle, making her think it wasn't *only* sex he wanted from her.

The idea of him making her a priority was such a sweet and heady thought that she nearly turned all mushy and cried. She wrinkled her nose at him instead and hurried him out the door. "You should get to work, then."

He stole one warm kiss and did.

# CHAPTER EIGHT

TRAVIS HAD FIBBED, Imogen thought on their last day in Hawaii. This hadn't been the affair they were supposed to have had. It had been the honeymoon she had longed for.

After a day of meetings in Honolulu and a mixer with his client, they had flown to Kauai and the site of a new resort Travis would build over the next three years.

He had booked them into a bungalow—which was actually a three-story six-bedroom villa with an infinity pool and a short walk down to a stunning lagoon. He had worked half days, taking her with him a couple of times to walk the property, have lunch with his clients and check out the competition.

The rest of the time they had floated in the pool, snorkeled in the lagoon or made love in the airy privacy of their palatial master bedroom. They drank excellent wine and ate fresh tropical fruit and other meals prepared by their day staff. It was bliss.

"I don't want to leave," she murmured when he joined her on their last evening. She stood at the rail of their private balcony wearing only a sarong, watching the sun set.

"Same." He stood behind her and set his hand on the rail near her hip, half caging her against it.

She leaned into his frame, utterly his after a week of near constant contact.

"Did you get your proposal sent?" he asked, kissing her bare shoulder and sending tingles down into her breasts.

She smiled and reached up to caress his jaw. "Are you asking if I got all my work done? I did. Not that I expect anything to come of it, but it was nice of them to invite me to throw my hat in."

"I don't think Nic does things just to be nice."

"Rowan probably does." Nic's wife had been on the hunt for a biographer for a couple of years, although not very seriously. She'd had other priorities with adopting children and other family commitments.

"The proposal makes a nice calling card, but I don't expect to pay the bills with writing. Not right away. I applied for some positions back in New York that I might actually get."

"Like?" His hand stole into the folds of her sarong. He cupped her breast, gently massaging so her nipple tightened and poked at his palm.

"Mmm…" She rubbed her hip against the growing press of his arousal. "Um…" She couldn't think when he did that. "Nothing inspiring," she managed to recall. "Scanning papers for a museum curator. I think the primary skill required is the ability to withstand supreme boredom."

She tried to turn, but he didn't let her.

"Don't lock yourself into something you'll hate." Her hair was up, so he kissed the side of her neck, then took her earlobe between his teeth, exerting just enough pressure to threaten pain, making her hold very still and grow sensitized all over, breast swelling into his hand.

"It feels good to take constructive steps," she said breathily, barely tracking that they were still talking. "I put my name on some lists for rent-controlled apartments, too."

His hand on her breast squeezed a little tighter before he shifted his grip and lightly pinched her nipple, circling and teasing and pulling.

"Let's go to the bed," she murmured, rubbing her butt into the front of his shorts.

"Not yet." His hand slid down her belly in lazy circles, caressing and building her anticipation until he slowly cupped his hand over her mound. He made a sound of satisfaction at finding her naked and slick. "I want to make love to you right here."

She bent easily to the light exertion of his frame against hers, until her elbows rested on the rail. She was already shifting her feet open, letting him touch her more intimately, biting her lip and scanning through slit lashes in the dark.

"Someone might see."

"There's no one here but us." He shifted to lift the back of her sarong away, then his strong thighs were against hers and he was probing for entrance.

Before they'd left New York, she had seen the doctor again and was fully protected now. She arched to take him in, gasping because she was a tiny bit tender. They made love constantly, but it felt so good every single time that she welcomed the friction against her sensitive tissues.

Even so, he made a noise of concern and moved very

gently, sliding his hand to caress her again where they were joined, exploring, inciting. Digging her nails into his forearm on the rail, she bucked and shivered with a sweet, quick orgasm.

His breath pooled at the top of her spine as he chuckled with satisfaction. "Again," he commanded, arousing her with easy thrusts and strokes. "This is all I think about all day, being in you like this, feeling you shiver and come apart."

"Me, too," she admitted, meeting the slap of his hips with pushes of her own. Her need for this made her desperate and scared. For all the steps she was taking to strike out on her own, she knew it was going to kill her to live without him. It made her greedy and uninhibited, determined to be whatever he needed.

When he covered her and held her tight, pressed deep and stroked her into losing herself, she abandoned herself to the pleasure he gave her, crying out, then whimpering with loss when he withdrew.

His shorts were already gone and he flicked her loosened sarong away with a single tug of one finger. As they stood there naked and bathed in the rising moonlight, he picked her up. Rather than take her to the bed, he took her to the lounger.

They stayed there all night, joined and caressing, kissing and pleasuring, neither wanting to go to the bed and end their last night in paradise.

Travis hadn't realized how much he'd grown used to coming home to Imogen until she wasn't there.

The short January days meant it was usually dark outside when he got home from work, but the main rooms were usually lit with lamps and the fire, and she was invariably cooking something that smelled mouthwatering, offering a kiss before getting back to whatever she was chopping or simmering.

It had been two weeks since Hawaii, and as of today, their affair had officially lasted one week longer than their marriage. He thought they should celebrate by getting out of the city and had reserved a cabin in the Catskills along with asking his pilot to fuel up and file a flight plan.

But the apartment was empty, the kitchen spotless and Imogen's laptop not winking a screen saver but completely off. She had had a lunch date with Rowan, but it was five o'clock.

He texted her and got a prompt reply.

Be there in twenty.

He poured himself a drink, surprised how much he wanted one. He told himself it was relief that she wasn't collapsed in the street again, but there was something about knowing she was on her way *back* that eased a tension inside him.

Did he wonder if there was a man involved in her delay? Maybe, but he consciously pushed that thought aside.

He didn't want to be jealous and dependent. He made a concerted effort *not* to be. It wasn't just left-over teenage angst from watching his father spiral. It was *her*. Along with wallowing in betrayal, he'd missed Imogen after she had left that first time.

That hadn't sat well with him. It was the reason he was trying so hard to keep his boundaries in place now. Hawaii had been incredible but had aided and abetted both a feeling of connection and of reliance. Not his style at all. *He* was the one who was needed, not the other way around.

He moved to look at the view, a place they often stood as they shared a drink, talking about their day. If she wasn't writing for one client or another, she went out on interviews and had signed up for a class to do some sort of website updating, so she would have more skills to peddle.

He found it strangely threatening.

She had also gone back and forth to his accountant's office, finalizing things for her father's estate, growing less stressed by degrees.

"I might actually be able to pay you back for his fee someday," she had said the other day. "Now that Dad's debts have been folded into his estate."

She had been tickled pink when her first earned income had gone into her account from a client of Joli's. It was writing blogs for a car dealership, the amount nominal, but a weekly thing she could count on for the next while.

"Look," Imogen had said, showing him the deposit on her phone. "I can take you out for a very modest lunch tomorrow."

He had opted for her to pick up sandwiches and deliver them to his office. They'd made love on his leather sofa. After she was gone, he had taken out the rings that somehow made their way into his pocket every day. *This could be my life*, he had thought. Imogen could be a fixture in his world, with her self-deprecating humor, delivering his lunch and erotic distractions, littering his home with shoes and hair clips, but filling it with her lilting voice and other signs of life.

*For how long?* he wondered. Marriage didn't last forever. Nothing did.

The elevator dinged and she came in, flushed and beaming, wearing the green dress he'd bought her the first day she'd been here. It sat tighter against her figure now that she was back to a healthier weight. Her breasts pressed against the neckline and the belt was no longer a loose bracelet around her waist but a pretty flash of gold that emphasized the flare of her fuller hips.

Fetching as she was, the way she kicked off her shoes and practically skipped toward him, looking very damned pleased with herself, was what really kicked up his heart rate. When she threw her arms around his neck and planted a big kiss on his mouth, her bright, golden energy coursed through him like a current.

He picked her up off her feet so her legs dangled and they were eye to eye, his arms around her butt.

"Did you finally win the lottery? Why are you so cheerful?"

"I'm always cheerful. But yes, I kind of did." She was incandescent, holding him rapt as he took in the sparkle of her eyes, the smile that wouldn't leave her lips, the air of sheer magic glittering around her. He wanted to make love to her, but he wanted to simply gaze on her at the same time.

"Where were you?"

"Rowan's. We finished lunch but weren't finished talking, so we went back to their apartment. She offered me a contract." Her eyes bugged out.

"For the biography?"

"Yes! I told her she was crazy, that there are other people who are way more qualified, but every time I tried to talk her out of it, she offered me more money."

"Why would you talk her out of it? That's fantastic. Let's celebrate." He walked them across to the wine fridge, then set her on her feet to bend and take out a bottle of champagne.

"I haven't signed anything. I wanted to talk to you first."

"As long as the compensation is fair, I say it's a terrific opportunity." He opened the cupboard and brought out two flutes. "Quit worrying you're not good enough. You are, otherwise she wouldn't have asked you."

"But I've never taken on anything so big. Nic has a guy working on his father's biography who's done seven already. I asked Rowan if I could cheat off his work. She laughed and said that's why she wants me. That we have the same sense of humor and she feels comfortable talking to me about her childhood. I guess her relationship with her mother was rocky at times. She needs someone she trusts to find the balance between truthful and kind."

He popped the cork and a minuscule cloud wisped from the neck of the bottle before he poured the frothy bubbly into the glasses.

"And she chose you. Well done. I'm proud of you."

Imogen hesitated to clink and he met her eyes. They were swimming in a thick gloss of tears. "Really?"

His heart took a swerve and nearly tipped completely. Had no one ever said they were proud of her? Ever?

"Yes." Emotion thickened his throat and his chest ached. "Very."

They touched glasses with a crystalline ping and sipped. Actually, she seemed to take a bigger gulp, swallowing audibly. Her voice sounded nervous when she spoke.

"There's a small catch if I take it."

*If.*

The air shifted. The pressure in his chest grew. "What's that?"

"I'll travel to Greece a lot, especially at first. She's fine with my bringing some things back here, but there's a lot to sort through. Letters and photographs. Playbills and other memorabilia. All very flexible. I'll be back for the opening of the hotel in Florida. If you still want me to be there." Her voice thinned as she said the last.

"You're leaving." And here came the train whistle in the distance.

"Rowan is taking the kids back to Greece at the end of the week. She's hoping I'll go with them, since she'll have some time to get me started while she's there. That's why I said I needed to talk this out with you first."

They hadn't made any commitments. He couldn't hold her back unless he was prepared to make one. He pushed his hand into his pocket and the diamond on the engagement ring cut into his palm.

"Once I sign the contract... The advance is very generous. I should be able to find a decent apartment—"

"Not necessary," he heard himself say, staring into the rise of bubbles in his glass.

"You don't feel differently about my being here, now that I have options?"

"No. I want you here." So badly it scared him.

Her mouth trembled into a fresh smile. "Really?"

The emotional intimacy of the moment nearly undid him. He hated feeling this vulnerable.

"Of course," he said gruffly. "Come here." He set aside his glass.

She moved into his arms.

He had to remind himself to be gentle, because the beast was roused. The greedy one who was possessive and ravenous and territorial, needing to mark her as his own.

She matched him, though. Matched him in the way that was terrifying because it turned their lovemaking raw and elemental, and because it told him she was feeling the same desperate need to cleave onto him that he felt with her.

He picked her up and carried her to his bed, leaving their fresh bottle of champagne to go flat.

# CHAPTER NINE

TRAVIS WOKE TO her cry.

He rolled, gathering her trembling form into him so her wet cheek smeared across his pecs. He was only half-awake, reacting on instinct, not thinking until he was stroking her hair and murmuring for her to wake up that she preferred to suffer through this.

He couldn't bear it, though. He couldn't bear the wrenching sounds of sorrow, and he couldn't bear the reason she was having her bad dream.

*When I'm feeling sorry for myself...*

Why? He had given her as much pleasure as he knew how to deliver, binding her to him as indelibly as possible without sewing their skin.

"Travis," she breathed on a sniff and hugged her arms around him, pressing her silky warmth to his front. Shudders of reaction were still working through her spine.

"My fault," he said in a voice that rasped his throat. They'd made love for hours, skipping dinner. "I'll go order something for delivery."

She made a noise that wasn't quite a protest, but the weight of her against him urged him not to move. Her heart rate eased along with her breaths, but she had a sense of despondency about her.

"I feel like this is the beginning of the end," she said in a hollow whisper.

He did, too, but he wasn't ready to face it. That's why he had drowned them both in sexual ecstasy. Cupping the back of her hair, he pressed a kiss to her forehead. "Let's see how things go."

He left the bed.

Imogen had been gone a week, and she missed Travis to the point she woke with a tearstained face and a dream of waiting for him to come to her, which he never did.

*I want you here.* She had taken such heart from that, but now she had time to reflect, she saw it wasn't words of love or commitment. What they had was unrestrained passion, not something that lasted.

So, even though she pined for him and feared that this job was going to be the undoing of their relationship, she also knew she had to push herself into a position of independence.

Heck, she needed that for her own self-worth and peace of mind. She could never stay with him as his mistress, kept and resented over time, eventually abandoned. She needed this job, this money, this distraction from fretting about their future. She needed to know she had a future regardless of what happened between them.

So she signed the contract and sent him a photo of her signature.

He FaceTimed her. "Congratulations." He looked so pleased for her that she could have cried.

"Thank you— Oh," she cut herself off, noticing the

man at the window. "Sorry. Rafe is waving and giving me a thumbs-up." She waved at him, calling, "Bye!"

"Who the hell is Rafe?"

She faltered under the sudden ice in Travis's tone. "I told you about him. He's my counterpart, working on Nic's father's biography. He's leaving for London."

"But he'll be back. You'll be working with him."

"Remotely. Travis." She had always thought that jealousy in a man would be flattering, but it just sounded like a lack of trust. "We'll check in via email, to discuss crossover details. That's all."

He seemed to accept that and she promised to come to him in Florida when she returned. He had a grand opening of a hotel he had designed and she was joining him for the gala ball.

She arrived with just enough time to change in their top-floor suite while reading his text that he was downstairs and couldn't get away.

He had left her a gown. It was an airy confection with a flowing skirt in shades that matched the tropical waters off their terrace. The bodice was strapless and snug, sexy and elegant at once.

She hadn't arranged a stylist so only gathered her hair back from her face, letting it fall behind her shoulders in a fluttering mass of auburn and amber.

When she arrived in the ballroom, it was an aquarium of bright gowns and tuxedos. She looked for a podium or the bar, somewhere he was likely to be standing—

*Oh.* He was looking right at her.

He held a drink and seemed arrested, wearing a look she couldn't interpret. Approval? Hunger? With a blink he took action, setting aside his drink and weaving toward her through the crowd.

Her heart soared as he approached. Growing bigger with each step until she couldn't deny what the enormous feeling inside her was. *Oh, no.*

"I missed you," she said, when she really wanted to confess, "I love you. I've always loved you."

It dawned through her with all the promise of a sunrise, a new day, a fresh start. It wasn't the immature, unrealistic love she had had for him when they were married, though. It was a mature, achingly wise kind of love that knew she couldn't beg for or demand or *earn* his love. She could only offer her heart and hope.

Was it glowing like a neon sign from her smile, beating like a telegraph message in her throat? He must have seen something because he seemed to grow more reserved. Stony.

"You look beautiful." He took her hand and bussed her cheek with the lightest of kisses, lacking the heated frenzy of need that thrummed in her.

The ballooning sensation inside her began to deflate.

"So do you," she said, trying not to falter into doubt. In so many ways, he had helped her find her confidence, encouraging her to pursue this job and believe in herself. She didn't want to think it was suddenly in jeopardy, but there was no safety net of reassurance to fall back on, no declaration of love, of anything, to save her from plunging into insecurity.

She kept her smile on her face and searched his expression, asking inanely, "Is everything going well?"

"Perfectly. I imagine you're tired from all the travel. You only have to make an appearance. Let me introduce you and you can disappear early if you'd like."

He took her cool hand in his and dragged her across to meet his clients. Words were said. Pleasantries exchanged.

"You haven't had a chance to look around?" the owner said, offering his arm. "Let me show you."

Travis offered his arm to the owner's wife and followed them onto the mezzanine. They looked down into the lobby fountain, then moved out to a terrace that overlooked a palm-tree-lined pool and a beach glowing in the moonlight against a starry sky. The design was meant to hark back to the owner's family château with arches and columns, wrought iron and well-crafted stonework. At the same time, his wife was very fanciful and demanded every luxury be afforded to their exclusive guests.

He'd seen it all and talked to these people until he was sick to death of them. He watched Imogen instead. Drank her up and hated himself for having waited to see her one more time before he ended it. Needing this much at least.

"It's stunning. Like a fairy tale castle," Imogen said after the tour. "And now I know your secret," she said to Travis in an undertone, hugging his arm. "You're a closet romantic."

He stiffened, reacting to her, as always. Applying brutal discipline within himself, trying not to.

He had been feeling her absence keenly, which unnerved him. He wasn't a needy man. It was uncomfortable for him to be distracted, wondering where she was, what she was doing. The hollow ache in him had warned of a deeper, more debilitating pain the longer their relationship went on. A harder fall when she left for good.

Then she'd delivered a one-two punch of taking a job that would continue to take her away and mentioning a man. The jealousy, the uncertainty, that had risen in him then had made it clear to him he was in too deep. He couldn't ride a roller coaster with this many plummets and heights. She already held too much power over him.

"Your husband is a genius," the owner stated magnanimously. "I couldn't be happier."

Imogen dropped Travis's arm, turning to correct the man about the state of their marriage, but his wife was busy saying, "You two should join us on the vineyard next week. We're having a house party at our cottage."

"Imogen is fresh in from Greece," Travis interjected. "She's writing a biography. I don't expect to see much of her in the next while as she digs into it."

His words jarred her. She glanced at him with a little frown.

She tried to keep a smile on her face as they returned to the ballroom, walking with the owner's wife now, telling her what she could about her assignment, but she kept glancing back at him.

When Travis drew her onto the dance floor, Imogen said stiffly, "If you didn't want people to think we're a couple, you shouldn't have invited me to join you here."

"I was repeating what you told me in your text," he said flatly. "You said you were going back as soon as you could. How is Rafe?" he added.

She stopped dancing. "What are you doing, Travis?"

"What do you mean?"

"You know." With a little flinch, she looked for an exit. "I'm not playing. Or maybe I am, because you don't really give me a choice, do you?"

"What the hell are you talking about?"

"I'm taking you up on your offer to leave early." She forced a smile. "Please make my excuses."

He looked into her eyes, the raw anguish and shadow of betrayal, and knew this was it. Wind seemed to rush past his ears, as though he was in free fall, but at least he could see the ground. The end point. *Okay, then.* He braced himself.

"I'll walk you up."

He followed her to the alcove where the bank of elevators let out. It was empty and a pair of doors opened the moment she jabbed the button.

"Why did you ask me to come down here?" she demanded as they were closed into a car alone. "Just so you could pull the pin in the most humiliating way possible? Why didn't you tell me to stay in Greece? Why did you tell me you wanted me to stay with you?"

"You're the one hiding that you're meeting a man—"

"Don't you *dare*." She charged out the opening elevators and down the silencing carpet of the hall. It took two jabs of her card to open the door to their suite, she was shaking so badly.

She barely restrained herself, waiting for the door to close before she rounded on him.

"Accuse me of anything," she said, rage thickening in her throat. "But don't you *ever* accuse me of cheating on you. You're the one who spent the four years since our marriage sleeping with anything that moved."

He rocked on his feet as though she'd clawed his face. "Bit late in the day to bring that up, isn't it?"

"You think because I haven't mentioned it that it

doesn't bother me? I hate it! But I have never once said anything because *I* left *you*. Our divorce was *my fault*. I was the villain." She knocked her breastbone so hard it thumped.

He frowned, but she railed on.

"No, I did not jump into bed with the first stranger I met, the minute I was out of your sight. Go to hell, Travis, for thinking I would." She kicked off her shoes and yanked out her earrings. She threw the jewelry onto the table, glad for the way her earrings caught in her hair. The hurt distracted her from the way she was disappearing inside. Growing hollow and filling up with darkness. "How many women have you slept with since I've been away?"

"None," he bit out, seeming affronted she would even ask. "But whether it was Rafe or some other man or some other reason, we were never going to last. You knew that, Imogen."

"Really?" That took her aback. "Well, I guess if you believe it, then it must be true."

He narrowed his eyes. "Your optimism is appealing, but it's delusional. We both knew, up front, that this was temporary."

"So Rafe is an excuse. You're ready to end it, but didn't have the guts to say so."

"Is there a reason this needs to be ugly? Yes," he said, voice brutally hard and clear as crystal. "I'm ready to end it. I'm sorry if that hurts you, but yes. It's over."

"Oh, you're sorry? *If* you've hurt me? Well, *I'm* sorry every day that I'm even *alive*. I've been conditioned to take the lion's share of blame in every confrontation or conflict. Do you realize that I'm going to walk out of here believing this was my fault? My fault *you* don't want to make a commitment. That *you* aren't capable of love. That *you* don't want *me*. You hurt me, Travis. Every single day, it hurts to be this in love with you and know you don't feel the same. Are you sorry for that?"

He flinched, jaw pulsing. "Yes. And it only proves my point. You should leave and find someone who can give you the love you deserve."

"Wow," she choked, thinking it ironic that she finally believed she did deserve it when he was telling her to look for it elsewhere. "I definitely will."

She hadn't unpacked more than her hairbrush and makeup. It only took a moment to fill and close her carry-on with a snap that sounded very loud in the thick silence. Like a gunshot through the heart.

"I'll get a few things from the apartment, then go back to Greece. Rowan set up the guest cottage for me to come and go." She lifted her head. "Don't expect me to stay celibate this time. Don't expect me to forgive you for the fact you won't. This is really it. This one is on you."

Travis went back to the party and only drank water, even though an urge to drink himself blind prickled his throat. He wasn't his father. He wouldn't be destroyed by a woman.

The next morning, he packed her gown and jewelry on autopilot, taking care of what needed to be done exactly the way he had every other time his life had taken an unexpected dip or turn.

He had told her the truth. This breakup was always going to happen. Maybe he had hurried it with his flare of jealousy, but even though he doubted she would ever cheat, the harder truth was that he couldn't *make* her be faithful. He couldn't *make* her stay.

He might not survive the disaster in the distance, so he had forced the issue today, while he was still able to carry on. He wasn't proud of it. Looking back, he saw he'd done the same thing the first time. His only regret was that he'd left Imogen feeling blamed back then. At least this time they both knew it was his fault.

Which was no comfort at all.

Rather than fly directly to his empty penthouse in New York, he stopped in Charleston to see his father. During Gwyn's escapade, Henry had moved into a gated neighborhood for privacy. Attention had long died down, but his father enjoyed the social community he'd formed there.

"How is it over when it only just started?" his father said after inquiring about Imogen. "I thought she was only going to Greece sporadically, not staying there."

Travis sighed, wishing his father would accept things at face value. This grotto behind his father's house was usually one of the most relaxing places to sit and visit with him, but Travis rose to his feet, restless.

"We knew very quickly the first time that we wouldn't last. We couldn't sustain it this time, either." He pushed his hand into his pocket and found her rings. He was going to ruin them, rubbing them together the way he constantly did, but he pressed them onto his finger and thumb tips, working them against each other. It had become a habit.

"I've been seeing your mother, you know."

"What?" Travis snapped his head around.

His father shrugged sheepishly. "We had coffee a

few days after my party. There were things we had
never talked through before. I hadn't given her a chance
to tell me her side of it, too busy calling her names and
impugning her. I worry I distorted your view of women
with things I said back then."

"Dad—"

"Do you know I was drinking before she cheated? I
never wanted to tell you that, but I thought you might
have guessed. No? It wasn't nearly as bad as after,
but I was feeling pressure from work. Untold pressure
from those committees asking me to run in state elec-
tions. Maybe I wasn't sleeping with other women, but
I was spending more time lunching with a bottle and
other people than with your mother. I wasn't there for
you the way I should have been, before or after." He
made a face.

"I'm not here to play blame games, Dad. I've never
felt that Mother really needed me, not the way you
did. That's the only reason I'm closer to you. We don't
need family therapy or anything." He rubbed the back
of his neck, thinking that felt like a lie. Maybe he had
come here looking for commiseration of some sort.
Women. Right?

"Has Imogen cheated?"

"Not even close," he muttered, freshly ashamed that
he'd questioned her about another man. She'd had every
right to be angry about that. "We're different people,
that's all."

"Good."

"How is that good? I want something I can count
on, Dad. Someone who's predictable, not..." Whim-
sical and kind and sensitive. Someone so sensual and
engaging he forgot himself.

"Then get a dog."

He shot his father a dirty look. "I don't want to believe we have a future, start a family, then discover we're not going to work. Better to nip that in the bud."

"If you actually aren't compatible, then yes. But what kind of lifetime warranty do you expect, Travis? Do you know what Gwyn said the last time she was here? That she was glad her mom had those years with me. We had plans, you know. We were going to travel. I was counting on *that*. It didn't work out, but I have no regrets. I didn't divorce her because she got sick and canceled our future. You can't count on anything, especially time.

"If you don't love Imogen, fine. Move on. But if you do love her, what the hell are you doing acting like she'll still be there when you wake up and realize you want her? You're wasting time you could be spending making my future grandchildren."

Travis returned to New York the next day. His father's words were turning over in his mind, wearing holes in his skull. Now his empty penthouse was filled with her memory, making it a difficult place to be. He called a Realtor and made an appointment, then stood in the office he had rarely used. He had intended to tell Imogen she could use this room as a home office, to write the biography. He stared at where she had lounged that first day, when he had fantasized about making love to her again.

If only he *had* got her pregnant that night on the yacht.

He pinched the bridge of his nose, wondering if that was what he was reduced to, needing the excuse of an unplanned pregnancy to try again with her. Really try.

Oddly, he was convinced that he would somehow make that work. He was at his best when he was needed.

He looked back on his father's breakdown, a time when Travis had been frustrated and angry but had understood his role. The few times he'd helped his mother, it had been when her lover was away and the sink had backed up, or she needed furniture moved. Gwyn had thought Travis hated her until her life had burned down around her. He'd been furious that it took her so long to involve him, thinking she ought to have known he would come the minute she asked, but she'd been too proud to fall back on him.

Was he waiting for Imogen to pass out in the street again so he could race in and save her? Had he felt threatened when she had ceased to lean on him? Had that been the real issue?

She had told him she loved him, but he'd only seen that she was leaving him despite saying it. She had said that he was hurting her, which had been a blow, one that had made him think letting her go was a kindness.

He hadn't considered that her upbringing predisposed her to have a specific need for love. He'd made no effort to meet that need. He had covered her basic survival with food and shelter—exactly as her piece-of-dirt father had done.

Travis didn't *want* to love anyone, though. He never had. Love was obligation and loyalty at best. At worst, it was an emotional wringer when the people you loved were in pain. Romantic love was a glittering facet of passion, not something true and deep and sustainable.

And yet, what he felt toward Imogen was all of those things. He knew that as clearly as he knew she had left him and it was nobody's fault but his own.

* * *

When Imogen had been a child, inventing stories had been her salvation. Later, when grief had engulfed her, she had filled up notebooks with poetry and song lyrics. Essays and ad copy and current events had all played their part in keeping her sane while her heart throbbed and ached.

Two weeks after her breakup with Travis, she had a new medium to help mend her broken heart, one she found infinitely fascinating because she identified with her subject. Cassandra O'Brien had been rejected by her family the moment her teenage aspirations turned to acting. She had had a rough life making ends meet, riding the feast or famine trials of acting, falling for men who didn't love her the way she longed to be loved—deeply and forever.

By some miracle, she had eventually met her soul mate and wound up here, on this Greek island, living in a house that looked like it belonged in the English countryside. It was a fairy tale and fed Imogen's starved, scorned heart with hope.

She couldn't help sighing over that.

"You sound like you've sprung a leak."

Travis's voice startled her so badly that she gasped and leaped to her feet, knocking her chair back into the wall.

He looked amazing. Rumpled and travel-weary in a button-down shirt with the sleeves rolled back, but a feast for her eyes as he gazed around the small front room of the guest cottage.

"Looks like you've called in Joli's decorator."

"I know. Rafe said this isn't how he works—" *Damn.* She bit her lip.

"Rafe," Travis repeated gravely.

"He peeked in the other day when he came by for some boxes. I don't see him. I shouldn't have brought him up."

Just like that, her eyes were hot and her self-worth was in the toilet. Tears were in her eyes.

This was why it was good they were over, she reminded herself. Not because he had accused her of cheating, but because he made her feel so very imperfect without even trying.

"What are you doing here?" she asked huskily.

"I want to talk to you. Can you take a break?"

"Travis—" She was barely hanging on over here, only getting through her days because the children checked on her and she refused to let them find her with her head in the oven. But there was no way she could withstand another interaction with this man. It could very well be the one that killed her.

She shook her head.

He closed his eyes, flinched. "I deserve that," he said in a serious tone that might have held an edge of agony. "But I came all this way. Give me five minutes. Please."

She looked around. The cottage was not only messy, but too small to contain him and how she felt about him. She couldn't risk permeating it with his memory. It would leave her incapable of living or working here.

"Outside." She cleared her throat and rose, picked her way across the piles littering the floor, each step a dreadful inch closer to more heartbreak. "We'll go to the beach."

He stepped back as she came through the door. She closed the screen and put on her sandals.

"Why didn't you call?" she asked as they made their way through the orange grove.

"Because you would have hung up."

Maybe. "Is something wrong?"

"Very."

She looked up, concerned. "Your dad?"

"You're here and I'm not."

"Travis—"

"I love you, Imogen." A flash of pain sliced across his expression as he said the words. "God," he muttered, rubbing the center of his chest. "I didn't know that would feel so good. I think I loved you when we were married. I think that's why I married you."

She halted, jaw going lax. "But you…"

"Let you go. Slept with other women. I know. I hate myself, Imogen. I hate myself for all of that. For hurting you. For calling you my only mistake. Letting you go was the mistake."

She tried to move her lips, but her hand was over her mouth and she didn't know what to say anyway.

"I don't want to be in love. I hate myself most for the tears that are coming into your eyes as I say that. But I need you to understand why it scares the hell out of me. I doubt you've slept with Rafe—in fact, I'm sure you haven't. But if you have, hell, I deserve that. I should have been true to you the way you were true to me. But it wouldn't change how I feel about you if you've been with a dozen other men. I don't think anything could. That's why I don't know how to handle it, Imogen. You *could* cheat and I wouldn't stop loving you. I would probably stay married to you. How the hell am I supposed to live with giving you that kind of power over me?"

He faced her and drew her hand down, holding both of hers in his. He was very solemn as he looked into her eyes. His were filled with turmoil and remorse and something so tender that the flimsy shields she'd spent the last two weeks trying to recover toppled like a house of cards inside her.

"How do I ask your forgiveness? How do I convince you, after driving you away *twice*, that you should give me another chance?"

Her heart was quavering so hard it turned her voice fluttery and weak. "Tell me again that you love me." Had she imagined it?

"I need bigger words, better ones, for what I feel for you. 'I love you' isn't enough. I've never been the one in a relationship who needs, but I *need* you, Imogen. I need you like air. I need the love you've offered me. I won't take it for granted again, I swear." His hands were tight over hers.

"Oh, Travis." She started to step forward, to throw her arms around his neck, but he disappeared.

He dropped to his knee and there in his palm were her rings.

She stacked her hands over her mouth again, this time to still the trembling of her lips. She was crumpling on all sides, wetness falling from her lashes as she clenched her eyes shut, terrified this was a dream and she was going to wake up alone.

"This time we do it right," he said. "A public engagement. A proper wedding with witnesses who will hold us accountable to our vows. I want to tell the world that you're mine, that I love you. I want you to let me take care of you because I want you in sickness and in health, Imogen. Richer or poorer. We've seen each other's worst. Let's do better this time. Let me have your hand. Please."

It was too perfect. He was saying all the right things and it wasn't *possible*. "I can't believe…" But she offered her hand because even if it was a dream, she wanted to take it as far as it could go.

"Believe it. You do deserve my love, Imogen. I'll do everything in my power to deserve yours." He reached for her hand and reverently slid both rings on her finger, holding her knuckles against his lips a long moment. "I've been wanting to see them on you… Never take them off again. Promise me."

He waited, looking as if he wouldn't rise until she gave him that vow.

"I do. I promise."

He rose and she shook even harder.

"Is this real?"

"It's very real. Feel." He pressed her ringed hand to his chest where his heart pounded inside his rib cage. When he kissed her, his lips were hot and worshipful. Then, because they could never resist turning a chaste kiss to a passionate one, they sank into a deeper kiss, one that tasted of hot blood and excitement, but something more exalted.

As they twined their arms around each other, desire rose, a desire that needed physical expression, but sought the joining of souls as much as bodies.

"We should go back to the cottage," she breathed, pulling back. Then she frowned, eyes widening in apprehension. "What about my contract—?"

"Sometimes we'll have to be apart." He said it with stoic dismay. "I'll come to you as often as you come to me. I don't want you to feel anything less than what you are, Imogen. My equal. My love. My heart. The woman I want to spend the rest of my life with. The woman I want in my life every single day. I love you."

"I love you, too, Travis. I always have."

"I know. You humble me with that. I want to give you everything your heart needs."

"You already have…"

# EPILOGUE

*Two years later*

SOMEONE WAS IN the bedroom, moving toward the bed. It wasn't Imogen. She was pressed against him, fast asleep. *He* was fast asleep, but even so, he was aware of this other presence and there she was. A girl who might have been Imogen at twelve with hair in two braids, the bridge of her nose freckled, her smile a little too big for her face and her teeth set with a hint of overbite. She was pretty, wearing a dress that might have been white or navy or the same red-gold as her brows and lashes.

One day, he found himself thinking foggily, he and Imogen would have a daughter who looked just like her. Maybe a few months from now.

She giggled. He heard it in his head along with her high, sweet voice. "He's a boy. I'm here to tell her not to worry about him. He'll be fine."

Imogen wasn't eating much these days and was worried her empty stomach was hurting the baby. Was she crying? Through his heavy sleep, he thought she might be starting to sob. He started to turn toward her and gather her in.

"Wait," the girl said. "I want to talk to her. I want to tell her I won't be coming anymore. She doesn't need me. She has you now. And Julian."

Who was Julian?

She giggled again. "If she's sad, tell her she'll see me when Lilith comes."

Who was Lilith?

"Go make breakfast. Be quiet. Don't wake her."

Travis snapped his eyes open to the walls of the penthouse. The blink of colored Christmas lights off the downstairs terrace reflected faintly on the ceiling. It was midmorning, Christmas Eve. He was fully dressed on the bed with Imogen. They'd been starting their day when she had been unable to stomach breakfast and started crying, fearful that if she didn't eat, she would miscarry. She was incredibly emotional these days, not feeling well at all, which was why they'd opted not to join everyone in Italy and were having Christmas here, just the two of them. Two and a half.

With his protective buttons pushed to max levels, he had cuddled her on the bed, promising to call the doctor, but they'd both fallen asleep.

Now she was whimpering beside him, face turned into the pillow, but it wasn't the sorrowful, lonely cry he'd heard before. It was a subdued sob, like she was trying to hold back her cries so she could listen.

His scalp tightened. It had been a dream, he assured himself. A bizarre, fanciful dream that had no place in a rational man's mind as anything but.

Still, he was very careful as he rose, letting her continue to sob. It went against everything in him, but he did it, heart battering his chest as he made his way down the stairs.

Such a weird day. It had started out so well, with the doorman sending up Imogen's author copies while she'd been trying to choke down breakfast. He'd teasingly put it under the tree with the rest of the wrapped boxes, earning a cry of protest from her.

She was *not* waiting until Christmas to open that one. For a woman who didn't celebrate Christmas, she was giddier than Toni about the prospect of opening gifts tomorrow. Today had been one of the happiest days of her life until she had become sick.

He picked up the book she had signed to him, the first out of the box. Flipping it over, he saw Imogen's smiling face—so like the girl in his dream, if older and more heart-catchingly beautiful. She had her elbow propped, her hand along her cheek so her rings showed. She wore three now, the original two with a third they'd had custom-made to match. They had decided three was the charm and so far, so great.

Her book was finished and advance reviews and pre-orders were strong. His latest project had been clinched by his wife's charisma, and they were expecting. Provided she was allowed to travel, they were headed to Hawaii in a few weeks for the latest phase of his project there.

He heard her stirring a few minutes later and put the finishing touches on the breakfast of toast and scrambled eggs he'd whipped together. He had already made her an appointment with the doctor, but she had time to eat first. Hopefully, it would stay down this time.

Her eyes were a little red as she appeared and she came right into his arms, fitting herself against him in the way that was reassuringly familiar. He rubbed her back, still disturbed.

"You were crying. I thought you must be hungry." He wasn't sure if he should mention his dream, but his gaze was drawn to the photo on the side table in the lounge. It was the only one she had of her with her mother and sister. Surely, he'd conjured the image from that.

"Juliana came."

He kept rubbing her back while the hairs all over his body stood up. "It's been a long time since you've had one of those." Not since before he proposed in Greece.

"She said she's not coming back. She says I have you now."

He cradled her closer, disturbed by the melancholy in her voice, but hoping this meant no more crying in her sleep ever again.

She drew back and cocked her head. "What do you think of the name Julian if it's a boy?"

"I love it," he said, voice catching with emotion, echoes of giggles still in his head. "Juliana if it's a girl?"

"I've always thought Lilith for a girl, after Mom."

"I like that, too." He was bonkers, no question, but he didn't care. Not when this woman made him so happy.

He hugged her and she smiled, lifting on her toes to kiss him.

He released her and she eyed the breakfast he'd made. "You're my hero for making this, but if the baby rejects it, that's not on me."

No, it would be on Julian.

Julian, who arrived seven months later with a fine cap of his mother's red-gold hair and a challenging but funny personality that kept his parents on their toes. Travis was so proud and filled with love for the boy, he could barely contain it. He wondered daily how he had ever thought this would be too much for him when he couldn't get enough of family life.

Their daughter, Lilith, came along two years after that. She had her father's coloring and a pair of eyes that Travis knew he'd seen in a dream once. She was incredibly sweet and loving, impossible to resist, not that anyone tried, especially her parents and brother. Her only flaw was a tendency to startle the life out of her father by appearing beside the bed in the middle of the night, then giggling at his reaction.

\* \* \* \* \*

# COMING SOON!

We really hope you enjoyed reading this book. If you're looking for more romance, be sure to head to the shops when new books are available on

# Thursday 27th December

# MILLS & BOON

## Coming next month

### THE SECRET KEPT FROM THE ITALIAN
Kate Hewitt

'Maisie.'

Antonio looked up at the sound of her name on another man's lips. The man was standing by the entrance to the hotel, a smile on his face as he held out his arms. Slowly Antonio turned and saw Maisie walking towards the man, a tremulous smile curving her lush lips, a baby nestled in her arms.

A baby.

Antonio stared as the man took the baby from her, cuddling the little bundle as he cooed down at it.

'Hey, sweetie.'

Jealousy fired through Antonio, although he couldn't even say why. So Maisie had moved on, found a boyfriend or husband, and had a baby pretty darn quick. That was fine. Of course it was. Except...

They'd spent the night together a year ago, and although Antonio wasn't an expert on babies by any means, the child nestled in the man's arms looked to be at least a few months old. Which meant...

Either Maisie had been pregnant when she'd slept with him, or had fallen pregnant immediately after. Or, he realised with a sickening rush, had become pregnant by him.

He hadn't used birth control. He'd been too drunk and emotional even to think of it at the time, and later he'd assumed Maisie must have been on the pill, since she hadn't seemed concerned. But now he remembered how she'd come to see him—how many weeks later? Two, three? She'd wanted to talk to him. She'd looked distraught. What if she'd been pregnant?

Why had he not considered such a possibility? Antonio retrained his shocked gaze on the man and baby, only to realise they'd already gone. Maisie had turned around and was walking back towards the ballroom, and presumably her waitressing duties. And his child might have just been hustled out of the door.

'Maisie.' His voice came out in a bark of command, and Maisie turned, her jade-green eyes widening as she caught sight of him. Then her face drained of colour, so quickly and dramatically that Antonio felt another rush of conviction. Why would she react like that if the child wasn't his?

'What are you doing here?' she asked in a low voice.

'I'm a guest at the dinner.'

'Yes, but...what do you want from me, Antonio?' She looked wretched, and more than once her gaze darted towards the doors and then back again.

'Let's talk in private.'

'You weren't so interested in doing that the last time we met,' Maisie snapped, summoning some spirit.

'Yes, I know, but things are different now.'

'They're different for me too.' She took a step backwards, her chin raised at a proud, determined angle. 'You didn't want to know me a year ago, Antonio, and now I don't want to know you. Doesn't feel very good, does it?' She gave a hollow laugh.

'This is not the time to be petty,' Antonio returned evenly. 'We need to talk.'

'No, we don't—'

'Maisie.' He cut her off, making her flinch. 'Is the baby mine?'

Continue reading
THE SECRET KEPT FROM THE ITALIAN
Kate Hewitt

*Available next month*
www.millsandboon.co.uk

# LET'S TALK
## Romance

For exclusive extracts, competitions
and special offers, find us online:

- facebook.com/millsandboon
- @millsandboonuk
- @millsandboon

Or get in touch on 0844 844 1351*

For all the latest titles coming soon, visit
millsandboon.co.uk/nextmonth

*Calls cost 7p per minute plus your phone company's price per minute access charge